THE TIMEHRIAN

THE TIMEHRIAN

ANDREW JEFFERSON-MILES

P E E P A L   T R E E

First published in Great Britain in 2002
Peepal Tree Press
17 King's Avenue
Leeds LS6 1QS
England

ISBN 1 900715 53 8

Prolegomenon   9

The Angel's Mouthpiece   25

Amalivacar's Exit from the Night Bush   83

To the great Guyanese artists
whose lives touch mine
Wilson Harris, Denis Williams
and Aubrey Williams;
and to my loving Geraldine.

PROLEGOMENON

This manuscript was placed in my hands by a visitor from Guyana. It is the legacy of a distant relative who took part in an ethnographic mission in the Guianas in the mid-Eighties and was believed drowned in a freak tide on the Atlantic coast of Guyana; but who, it now appears, lives.

The inscription, "For my cousin AJM", tells me that his testament was destined for me, and curiously it arrived at a time I was making dream notes on the native imagination and its arrival in the poetic memory. These rapidly turned into questions the manuscript raised as I was reading it. Its residues of memory roused a parallel in my own person of a parable of history in a new, unknowing psyche. I can only compare it to being written upon by discontinuous histories which, when viewed through the native imagination, afford me an unusual and compelling perspective.

In this premonitory dream of history, crossing continents and civilizations, I perceive the deluge and submersion of Manchester village, East Coast, Guyana, as the actualisation of Kaer-Ys, the low-lying, then buried harbour of Celt myth. I find in

9

my cousin's manuscript a new-buried harbour and new-emerging compass of our times reappearing in the Guianas.

In the Celtic legend of Ys or Kaer-Is, the Low City or City of Below, King Gradlon of Cornwall returns home from war in the North with a magically beautiful woman, a kind of Nordic fairy. On the ship home, a girl, Dahut or Ahes [Ahes/Alc'huez *key*], is born out of the sea and the fairy dies in labour. The girl grows supernaturally quickly, wins her father over and becomes his new consort before they reach land. In her desire to return to her birthplace in the sea, Dahut-Ahes persuades Gradlon to build a city on low-lying ground. A tidal wave comes and claims the city. Dahut stays in the below-sea, Gradlon on the above-ground.

Within its shell or explicit meaning, the legend contains a latent reference to deluge and drought: a city built on land but eventually lost to the sea points to its continuance on the ghost of dry land. From a landed perspective, the inhabitants of the submerged city enact a ghost constituency of submerged land: they literally ghost dry land.

A ship that acts as birth-cradle to a creature of the sea indicates that the man-king did not sail an ocean so much as navigate a warning or premonition of drought. The fairy and the sea are psychic equivalents: the sea//fairy dies in labour to be resurrected later in the tidal wave. The king's ship is a latent drought ship in so far that as the fairy nears Gradlon's kingdom it moves her closer to her death. Her inexorable distancing from the sea sets up a drought condition in the legend to bring about her death.

England's Celtic prehistory reappears in contemporary Guyana in what is shared between the now-disappeared coastal village of Manchester & environs and its now-estranged seat, Manchester-Kaer-Ys, below the brown, esplumed lines of the Guyanese Atlantic. The legend of submerged Kaer-Ys is a ghost architecture to the events at Manchester village. Celtic Kaer-Ys has, no doubt, been carried round the world to be visualised in other oceans and inundated cathedrals.

In a manner of speaking, the Atlantic coast of Guyana is both sunken sea and drought bed. In a former geological age, the now-populated strand of coastal villages and towns was the bed of an ancient sea that reached up to fifty miles inland to its ancient shore, a sandy plateau rising swiftly into highlands.

Certainly, in the inverse sense that the inhabitants of ancient Breton Kaer-Ys ghost dry land, on the coast of the Guianas, one walks, one lives, on the former bottom of the sea; one land-navigates a ghost of former water, and there is something of this cross-over in the fiction where, following on the tidal wave, my cousin felt himself become a miraculous lung who waits for, then evades, rescue.

In the tidal wave which claimed Manchester village, part of my cousin escaped above ground, just as another part became dislocated in the tidal reaches; part of him abiding with rescue from an undisclosed location, part of him submerged in a compass of relocated seeing. As I read, I recognise that the deluge was not the absolute end of Manchester village but that there is a going forward and backward in composite being.

Strands radiate out of Celtic Kaer-Ys to Manchester village; rays from the future and the past, a non-absolute quest I have to accept and somehow accommodate. I have to recognise how my cousin's dying compass heralds the differing layers and weightings and periodicities of his life as a rehearsal that is still going on. What he writes makes manifest his acceptance of that rehearsal as a marvellous opportunity to suspend closure, preclude determinism.

Unconscious contradiction, housed as disquieting rifts in the individual community and the composite self, can sabotage the best intentioned and conscientious studies of the family of man. Rifts in a particular community may suggest a re-composition in the wider body of civilisation that in new ways sensitizes us to our unborn selves; selves that have stayed lodged in seemingly intractable histories and personal circumstances.

I believe the arts of the imagination have the capacity for apprehending such things and sensing human life suspended in the web of creation as but one more instrumentality in the parable of being.

I am, you might be gathering, possessed by invisible institutions: possessed in the sense that my imagination plays host to the multiple forms through which civilisations define themselves: vessels of myth, sacred writings, ethnologies and festivals; celebrations of the culture in artistic form.

There is a temptation to shape these institutions into the histories of specific peoples so that those peoples become survivors of a victimising lineage. The conventional view of history tries to coerce a person such as my relative into unstated victimhood, yet the empirical evidence culled by the ethnographic team points elsewhere. What I am suggesting is that our attempts to conserve mass-hierarchies often take place at the expense of others. Eventually, provisional attempts at conservation will precipitate the breakdown of symmetrical or monolithic stances; the very models our world wishes to preserve.

My obsession has long been to ask, how are we to reach a more open conception of ourselves?

If we turn to the Americas we see that they are unique among the inhabited continents of the globe. The ancient Americas offer recent and compelling example of what might befall the family of man once it leaves the Earth and starts to populate the stars.

Let us start with the anomaly: man is not native to the New World. No apelike primates from whom man evolved have yet been found in the Americas. There are no great apes or proto-human species, living or fossil, in the Americas.

This must be contrasted with the discoveries of Neanderthal Man in Rheinland Germany, of "Lucy" in the East Rift of the Upper Nile, of "Abel" in the West Rift, of Java man, and Peking Man in other inhabited continents. The Americas, then, are, to our current knowledge, a continent of "introduced species". That landmass fosters a laboratory of Man, the non-native species, a biosphere of introduced humanity. Layers of history and environments in the Americas allow us to discern how our own sowing of the stars and galaxies in the future might root us and displace history. As seedlings for the stars, the globe might well look at ancient America to see how the human species behaves on non-native ground. Is it not sobering data? Human predation and sacrifice as an instinct for life among the ancient Maya and Carib over other First Peoples. Then the coming of the New World and the eradication of entire civilisations in an eye-blink (Peru and Mexico collapsing in the dozen years between 1519 and 1531) so that hundreds of years would have to pass before either region would approach the population and prosperity it had achieved at the start of the 1500s.

Once we quit this globe, our nursery-bed of the stars, we will encounter species of whom we know nothing and who know nothing of us, and who might well remain outside our conceptual pool. How will we cope?

It is in ancient America that unique meetings between men of different civilisations, with no previous knowledge of one other, most recently took place. The instances that followed the first half of the 1500s, contemporary with us and with which we have become more and more pregnant, attach to a womb already complex with layers of history and environments in such a way that the events of the recent centuries are further inducements to alter our fixed perceptions of one another, from one of the rigid monolith of appearances, into a consciousness of how the hidden residual self will ambush or undermine such appearances.

As particular instance, Guyana is a self-named, self-styled land of six peoples: indigenous Amerindian, African, East Indian, Chinese, English and Portuguese. As an open-ended demographic envelope, Guyana promotes a heterogenous vision of community. It is, I know, in a special sense, a privileged conception, and one that makes of Guyana a privileged space. The two European peoples supplied the earliest indentured workers (Portuguese) and administrators (English); from the middle of the last century Oriental peoples (Indian, Chinese) made the second wave of indentured workers, whereas African peoples were first slaves then the very last wave of indentured workers. The indigenous peoples, some of whom were unsuccessfully coerced into the earliest forced labour, are vestige-neighbours of a once-massive Amazon basin civilisation that numbered in the eight to nine millions in the 1540s and which, two centuries later, were reduced by sponsored purges from the Iberian peninsula to produce *limpiados* or ethnically-cleansed territories. Thus according to a conventional or *half-mile* reckoning, to a history that enacts itself according to the monoliths of victors and victims, in Guyana, peoples indigenous and immigrated share a common disinheritance and internal exile rooted in a shared geographical space.

The territory of the Guianas constitutes a northern operculum or lid in mainland South America. It covers the region from the Atlantic coast to the Amazon basin and holds the continent's rainforest. The Guianas are the breathing gill and lung of the Americas. In recent history, it may be thought of as an *immigrated-space* into which peoples, often from incommensurate cultures and ethnicities, have been imported from other continents, turned to segregated labour, then in the aftermath of independence, left to mix up with one another. The premise of such an experiment seems to be that the space, once populated and subjected, will continue the conventions of the nation state.

It goes without saying that there can be no such conventional issue. The lives of indigenous peoples prior to the immigration of modern times and the appearance of my cousin's new unknowing self, and its harrowing of what he had been, point to a pathology of eclipse in civilisations and to the deforming of history into events accomplished by greater and lesser personalities along the linear historic line.

What is being composed in my cousin's narrative seem to me to be in the nature of *giornati* or sections of a day, like fresh applications of paint worked in singular session on a discontinuous fresco. The *giornati* I am discovering here are superimpositions of diverse origin allied to and alloyed with the interrupted and ruptured masquerade then Mass at Manchester, and which now continues its singing in Kaer-Ys Citadel Below Manchester.

At the heart of institutions we take as our given means – the finite number of celebrations hidden and apparent, the feasts and festivals of memory and remembrance: formal mainstays that hold the definitions of the culture-in-form – exist vestiges of diverse custom as abjected traditions that infiltrate and subvert our acts of office and cognisance and so manumit the substance of the known thing into new substantials. Such older and more archaic customs may reappear in ways that seem alien, or approach from an unaccustomed future by which we have yet to place ourselves, comparatively, side by side.

An alertness to this sharing of mutual space can precipitate us into community with our neighbours. We become alive again with the spirit born of the trials of the past and the custom or framed cultural reflex which attempts to retrieve the past by way of cultural institution (Eucharist, fete, public holiday, ecclesiastical calendar, historic dates) may find that the myth of a continuous historic line is constantly subverted and newly colonised by latent and repressed traditions or identities in those diverse peoples. My cousin points out, for instance, that in Manchester Village the traditional Christmas Eve Service (the Magnificat) is preceded by eleven o'clock masquerade. The figures *in mascera* carry, self-evidently, the residue of Christian syncopes: the Long Lady's overtones of the Virgin; the Donkey Man's undertones of Christos; the Whistling Man's *sousentendu* of Satan, and the Rice-Doll, plaited and attached to the eaves of houses, the elevated, resuscitated body; and behind them marches a phantom band of reconstitution, a flute-band with terrifying or eleventh-hour associations with pre-Christian and extra-Christian practice. I remember reading that the archaeological rubble at sites such as Lachish in the Fertile Crescent contained upper thigh and hind bones and that these were payment-offerings made of many animals by the grateful Israelites to their priests, who instructed: "Give the right hind-leg of your shared/payment-offerings as a contribution to the priest" – *Leviticus* 7:32. "Any earthenware vessel in which the payment-offering is boiled must be broken; if it has been boiled in copper, that must be scoured and rinsed with water. Any male of priestly family may eat of this offering, it is most holy." – *Leviticus* 7:28-29. The flesh of the upper thighbone is boiled. If I tell you that the chosen people copied from the defeated Canaanites and their Temples of Baal these customs or habits into the framed cultural reflex of sacrifice, this would still be only a portion of the injuncted feast. If we consider also that in the South American continent at the same era, B.C. 1,200, the Carib offshoot of the Maya were beginning their conquest of the island-range they give their name to, and that their sacrifice also aimed at the boiling of the flesh of the upper thigh – but of captured human offerings – it allows us to surmise that the Israelite sacrifice in animals ghosts a memory of previous Canaanite sacrifice of children, the old and the infirm. It does not end here. The Carib did not discard the thighbone. They hollowed it into a bone-flute to play upon and reconvene the skeletal body. Thus the peoples transported from the African continent, who began to practice belief-institutions such as limbo, cumfah and obeah on the South American mainland, masquerade a Whistling-Fluting Man and a Flute-Band. It is as though, having been displaced into a traumatised, populated limbo-space, they dug down into layers of the continent and, in place of the recuperated bones of ancestors, found, instead, a shared or payment-offering in hollowed-out thigh bones and attempted (as recomposed skeletal bodies in masquerade) to redeem the bone-flute by the masquerade's position before the Christmas Eve Mass.

Thus exists a disturbing congruence and anastomosis of peoples remote and unconnected by any continuous historic line. Yet despite the absence of contingent or causal history, there exists the blatant congruence we note above. Cross-civilizationry anastomosis. Capillary meshing of peoples and their acts. The ark which beaches on Mount Ararat is an earth-fated capsule in which communities in crisis embark for prolonged gestation and, hopefully, re-genesis. The Celtic king, Gradlon, builds a city on lowland he must intuitively know he will have to surrender to the sea – as if his was a maritime

19

architecture and bridge to a composite and discontinuous self.

That composite self might gauge with man's eventual dis-closure with Time: eternal cities destined to rise forever from death and ashes, the fall then resurrections of Beirut, Baghdad and Saravejo making explicit their intuitive translation with deathless Jerusalem.

My cousin writes of his narrative as an act of restitution. Restitution is in the nature of deed-epigraph. OE *daed*, akin to OHG *tat*, Goth *gadeths*, an act effected by the imagination, and Gr. *epi* + *graphein*, to write upon, literally a writing-above or superimposing of one text over another, so that two texts of distinct provenance are meeting and re-reading themselves mutually, the one through the other, into a paradoxical pericope; a self-designation with one's composite being. I look at my cousin's deed-epigraph not as a record of the deed but the deed itself.

And the Timehrian. Who is the Timehrian? The Timehrian, I deduce, is one involved in what I shall call, in a special sense, the memory of oblivion. To reconstitute memory from lapses in oblivion is not just to make emerge the forgotten, but in a telling sense, it is to compose, for a first time, the paradox of memory. There is a latent constitution, not just in the explicit sense of the formal arts of memory such as allegory, parable, myth, legend, cabbala, semiots and symbols to which we may or may not retain partial keys over historical time, but memory's hidden ground, which is connected to the native imagination in revolutionary ways I am only just beginning to fathom. One such sense is that it enables our arrival at a memory of oblivion: it enables the arrival of memory's own paradox. Thus the amnesiac and the individual of plural cultural origins partake of a shared legacy: both must work out perspective from fragments; both must recuperate latent connection unexpectedly allied and alloyed with discontinuous histories or hinging instances across civilizations that share hidden kinship. Quite independent of shared history, I am discovering that such kinship is rife between Europe and the Americas. The changeling-boy, from whose fleeting hand my cousin received an *impresia* on New Year's Day, nineteen hundred and ninety-one, in Wismar-Mackenzie market, seemed to designate an origin whose uncanniness broke my cousin's loss of memory and prompted him to begin his book of paradigm, by which I mean the showing of the one thing side by side another that is otherwise hidden or submersed. For just as the everyday is clothed in the augmented womb of relocation that is cosmos, so one is divulged and remodelled in man's masking of the diminutive, divined entity of the self called anthropos.

AJM
in response to questions raised
in a dream note written in the nineteen nineties.

THE ANGEL'S MOUTHPIECE

74A The Government Housing Scheme
Wismar, Demerara, Guyana.
Restitution.

Dear Cousin,
I am the hypothetical survivor of the High Mass
and masquerade feted and sung on Christmas Eve
nineteen eighty-four in the village of Manchester
on the coast between New Amsterdam and the
Courentyne in Guyana, South America.

We Guyanese acknowledge, matter-of-factly, that
the coastland is below sea-level and that the only
natural disaster to be feared is flood. The conservation plan for the Canje-Courentyne water table is
today still on the drawing board, yet the absence of
a flood-control infrastructure in coastal areas cannot wholly account for the tidal wave which took
the entire village, two thousand inhabitants, and a
nine-mile stretch of coast into the sea.

I narrowly escaped with my life and a fiery
tongue of the sun I inadvertently swallowed and
which consumed my memory for the next six solar
years. Overlooked in the rescue attempts, I was able
to withdraw, unnoticed, upcountry then cross-
county to Linden-Mackenzie, Demerara to reconstitute myself.

It was a journey made on foot through the backlands of Berbice, the inland decayed forests of the Mahaica-Mahaicony flood system, the Demerara watershed of forest, sandhill and savannah. There is no ready-made path through these places. It is a spectral dream-country of places visited and never returned to exactly again. Was it then I first inclined to the notion that I might be criss-crossed and traditioned in ways I barely suspect?

Innocently, I inherited a spiritual estate, the hidden origins of which I was ignorant. I lived one conscious way, unaware that my residual gestures, speech, inflections, and heart were turned another. I spoke words, made sounds that were subtly contradicted by my residual movements and inflections. That residue confused others, who in turn wrong-speeched me with their own confusion. In this way was articulated a hidden language that suspended me in a compassless ark of providence.

For my crossing-over journey from the Canje coast to the Demerara River interior, I borrowed the back trails and bush routes and had to depend on others for food. When asked by my hosts what I was and the details of my provenance, I said that I was a 'shipper', for what stuck in my mind, a mind pellucid with the loss of personal memory, was the 'ships' or jewelled alignments in the mariner's compass, a compass I have no recourse to, yet which seemed somehow to ghost navigation in my ark of memory.

The tidal wave that swept all away possessed a sort of hybrid vigour that reached over our best attempts at correction. It exhibited an evenhanded kind of intervention in our affairs, entangling and suborning layers and institutions and environments. Former legacies are converted into new bodies whilst old shapes enter the squall and masquerade of memory, whose disguises enact majestic instability in our conception of ourselves. It is a complex, a charged phenomenology of practice and custom intensifying communities diverse in their origins, orientations, dictions.

The trauma I suffered in Manchester made me a candidate for rescue but instead I hid myself, partly in shame of my likely consolidation into plot or premature closure, partly because I feared the language of rescue would continue to perjure a speech that might, eventually, bring itself to acknowledge its own unfinished miscegenation.

Not all died in the sudden compression. Agile children and otherwise steady and reliable women and men who survived the first wave, dived below the flood and stubbornly submerged themselves again when delivered back to the surface – the number of dives in odd numbers, the number of redeliveries to infiniteness in even.

Leon-Battista Mondaal is my painted-with-all-colours name.

The Amerindians of the Guianas understand the *timehr* to be one who makes marks in creation with the hands, paints with the gods' hands, omens with colour the way *I* am being omened.

I was the literary figurist in Jacob Laban's team for Cultural Survey. It was my business to make into personal testament the proceedings of what was part of a global research project in the definitions of culture. As part of that comprehensive, ongoing survey in human self-gnosis, our team was assembled in nineteen eighty-four to record the Christmas Eve masquerade of Manchester village, in a vestige-tradition enduring from the Nineteenth century. We set up our ethnographic mission in the schoolhouse of Manchester village.

My own name, Leon-Battista Mondaal, hints at a renascence fragmented in our times into notions of the flowering of prominent civilisations, such as the new civilization-making taking place in the circum-Caribbean today. My name inspires in me a curious half-half baptism. It acknowledges ideas of the universal in the spirit of man at the same time as it bears on imaginative traditions with links to a new exploratory figuration of History; a harrowing of ground so that the histories of the eclipsed and the forgotten, those whose ways of living are dark-sided in the shadow/composite of history's giants, can emerge.

It is a form of comprehensiveness that becomes necessary in an age where micro-technology is aimed at the construction of virtual space as the diminutive rehearsal for the great spaces and future biospheres of the planetary systems.

Dark gross eclipse is made by the giant person-alities in whom we frame history. So much of pertinence is made to disappear. So much gets subjected, occluded, prevented from speech – though is the fact of occlusion not in itself a kind of telling?

The trauma I suffered from the day of deluge 24 December nineteen eighty-four continues me at the epicentre of the tidal bloom and the flood-race of bodies spiralling with submerged Manchester village and final descent. I am culpable because I did not take risks to even the odds that favoured ca-tastrophe. Although our cultural survey was not the direct cause of the catastrophe, there was undeni-able catastrophe in our method and I cannot help but draft a connection between the advent of the tidal wave and the character of our study.

In the flood and the turbulence, the disfigured masks worn by the *benthos* or deep-sea bodies be-came unstable and loosed from their fascial fixtures and, coming free of their lapsed performers on the sea bed, began transferring to and investing my own surviving person. So I began to wear, and continue to this day to wear about my hidden person, a new mesh of faces, my buffoon refigurement, my masks of reconfiguration.

I have already implied that our act of studying what appeared to us a self-contained system constellated that system in a falling down of stars, a disaster that seemed the twin of the hidden configuring of Laban's team.

Conventional epistemes for the study of man (social relativism in anthropology, ethnolology, ethnography) tend to benefit least those about whom the study is made. Those about whom the study is made rarely get to participate in it. They do not choose the people who measure them. They have no say in testing the soundness of the human instruments that measure them. Is it not a first principle, to be sure of your instruments, their origin, their proofing, their compatibility with the task; how much more so when that instrument is the human organum?

Did our native host – village and villagers who prepared the cataclysmic Christmas Eve masquerade – become sensible to *our* act of study or formal measurement? Did familial concepts of kinship, historic causality, demographic labelling and societal assessments of progress become truly *in*expert? This human biosphere, this temporal ark and fable of the future, what technically I will call the Manchester interpretation of cultural institution, would emphasise, in hindsight, the ineluctable participation of the actual measuring apparatus used – a notation I am shortly to outline – in determining value. Did we omit to include this notation or *méchanisme démesuré* as part and parcel of the result? Why did our studious experiment not become sensible of this omission?

I should start by confessing the complexion of my feelings for our group leader Laban; for he was a contemporary colossus whose intellect and personality were earmarked, yes, whispered and mooted, to figurehead the age.

I know that my gradual recognition of how much I feared Laban, and the mutilation in the historical fabric that the veneration of such a figure brought, pitched me into a kind of systemic shock from which I did not feel able easily to recover. I housed, in secret, the compressed rage, helplessness, and broken-winged, keeling, providential knowledge I felt. Laban's inner circular court or *tondo* made of me a guiser constricted and subordinated to an overall consensus I should have had the honesty to resist and reconstitute. Coerced into a particular perspective of myself, into a convention of seeing myself; that round, edgeless picture of myself, once admitted, became self-evident, causally inevitable.

By the time I encountered him, Laban already wore the mantle of fame and was crown prince of global historicism. He was a charismatic fiction of a man come full-bodied to the masquerade of life. He had it in his power to make international committees bow their head to catch his words in their ear. It was in his remit to knit or to make-slip careers. Grant-giving foundations ate from his hand and fed from his pocket. Laban had independent wealth. Some would say he was a giant to whom I just did not measure up. What I did do was to allow the hidden yet explicit compass of Laban's inner circular jestery to continue to mummer against its own implicit indirection. Unwittingly, the methods of the Team for Cultural Survey switched, in a sense, the polarity of the entire nine-mile stretch of coast between Rosehall and Salton (including Lancaster, Liverpool and Manchester villages). Psychically, those attitudes were a hiding away of the magnificat of mud-flat, silt and brown ocean alongside which lived the two thousand lives that were taken in the flood.

Now this is not a fact I can state in any absolute sense. It is a notion that engages my humanity, my conscience. In writing this account, I seek to recompose the cast-work of characters in which dismantled pulmon I am breathing a new living breath of memory in deposits of silt and new mud from which the flood is finally beginning to subside and marches to form.

When I escaped from the floodwater I hollowed out a hole in my own outline in a mudbank and warmed it dry with the heat of my body, lisping in and out of harrowed sleep. In this manner of being, I slipped into the bush and lay on the ground as though encased in an iron-lung of relived drowning and resuscitated rescue.

Slumber occupied a series of frames always slipping open so that it paradoxically promoted themes of dismantling for a later healing reconstitution. It is in just the same way that the new fertility implicated in flood makes it not wholly a fable of punishment and destruction, but might cocoon immanence and embodied multitude for when my book would eventually dream me and its writing.

Helicopters came but little would have been visible from aboard the wings of the sun. Pairs of seaplanes alighted but soon flew off again for there was no visible human salvage to be made.

In finding no bodies to recover, the dispatch then subsequent recall of help displaced me into a watershed/flood-shadow environment perpetually beyond absolute rescue and this fixed, I believe, the seal of confession on what I call my heterotic self-inscription.

One such seal or harrowing-band – it came to me as I was carrying the idea of heaven down into the abysmal inflorescence of my mud-weave – is the flood notation I use. That notation – my ark of survival – helped me to weather the destruction of my ready-made picture of the world and the six and more years I was soughing out numbing water from my lungs at the same time as being committed to the amnesiac's swimming strokes and their ter-rible sustained control. In my place of convales-cence, the mining township of Wismar-Mackenzie up the Demerara River, I was able to find an inner position along the open-caste lineage of peoples who lived by both banks. The Bank of Chirality or evenhandedness, as in the deluge at Manchester, was also here at Wismar-Mackenzie, my place of convalescence, located on the Wismar side which, along with the Bank of Classical Limit (the Mac-kenzie side), constituted the visible boundary lines, though other benchmarks were exerting a chronic, though hidden influence. Geological fault lines crossed and buckled cultures apparently distinct and separate. There was a strange covenant between the biblical, the nation state and the immigrated space. These meetings are usually hidden because they are compacted from view; and it was among the ridges and contours of these collapsed dimensions – hidden, according to Laban, within the first few instants of all new creation – that I was able to locate an inner anastomosed or cross-connected composition of the self.

What else survived outside the Manchester Ark? In hindsight it does not seem likely that my survival could have been the only possible outcome. The part of me which no longer exists (time's passage) might also be lodged in places other than the closed past. In what kinds of space should I search for the non-existent?

When my book began to dream me and its writing on New Year's Day, nineteen hundred and ninety-one, I was taking part in an agglomerate yet strangely integral Independence gathering and its complex yet lucid massed-march. It took place in the mining town I had settled in for my restitution six years previously. The convocation was along Half-Mile Road, a bauxite-surfaced track that ran on the Wismar-side of the Demerara River from Mackenzie Rail & Road Bridge to the graveyard at Christianburg, and from Christianburg back to Mackenzie Bridge, to and fro, backward and forward, like a de-railed track which once ascended up and descended down from heaven.

I joined a massed-march that I first became aware of as a boy of fourteen on Guyana's Independence Day when it passed through the Wismar-Mackenzie mining township, and which now, twenty-five years later on New Year's Day nineteen hundred and ninety-one, was finding a masquerade-role for me that would no longer disfigure, and I could lose myself in a crowd as one might lose a figure of clothing or mask of speech in masquerade.

Let me begin at the moment I slipped out of Laban's frame and he shoved me in what I now know to have been a limb-room of psychical re-proportion.

The clarion clearness of the water was deformed – a compacted sinnet cord of individually vibrating strings – my head like a broken-off capstan falling from the deck of the wave and plunging with the deep's sinoidy. The inflorescence and the brown water made me suppose the fall and immersion of a certain number of stars that, paradoxically, remained diminutive, as if hiding collapsed dimensions.

In the orchestration of the deluge, Laban danced with cutlasses as if to hew and trim at the tree of life while still rising in its branches. His cutlasses were balanced as if in the intense concentration of sculpting waxen effigies of a Jacob's struggle with angels, so that my words to him got stuck like flight-feathers affixed in wax to the fleshed and winged blades of his plunging shoulder, though when I attempted to speak he indulged me.

"We live, Leon-Battista, in spectacular connection with waves and ourselves. We signal to one another with them. Think of the metaphors, 'I wave you hello'; 'I wave you goodbye', 'You wave back', 'You wave me on'. We code our own cultural undulation when we speak of the 'The New Wave' in the imaginative arts. Then waves provide us with approximative concepts: theories and theatres of motion and of irradiation. Waves riddle our bodies and our feelings. We speak of having 'waves of emotion', of being 'at a peak' or 'in a trough'."

I stopped mid-stroke to try to accommodate what Laban was saying. I oscillated between a sense of congested rage (waxen rage which received the impression of violent emotion) and real engagement with the matter of his statements. It was true that man was a spectacle of waves, that man was spectacular with wave motion – my own alternations of rage and wonder especially full of wavelike character.

Without ceasing to dance, Laban turned as if to see me for the first time. His cutlasses twitched and the blades seemed suddenly to giggle as if tickled. Moonlight shone from within a prismatic labyrinth when I tilted my head toward the steel's lustre.

Why was Laban still in life when so many had already drowned? His continuance was a grotesque offence to what I felt were the limits of decency. His appearance in the prow of the Manchester Ark made mockery of me for I saw that he would not trouble to attempt my rescue from the flood water. The Judges of the Dead had withdrawn to a hidden, crescented chamber in the Moon while the Advocates of the Living were still making their unhurried way through the night-bush. It would be some hours before they would reach the outer edges of the rice fields behind Manchester village. I was on my own.

The lung of water in which I lay, my single coelum-lung, now heaved with a new-found precariousness. It was both rheumy and hollow and in the numbing cold the supply of air was cooling and condensing and loosing droplets like surprising seeds. Yet I knew that all living things were in the ark and the seed of all living things too. My lung began to keen for this.

"Oh my!" the lung keened.

I turned over in the water to rest the lung. Floated for a while with my belly up. Steered with the rudder of the spine in the sunken meadows and wet-charnels of Manchester.

The lung ceased its pleurisy yet continued to articulate mute phonemes in the warm air of the night for the bloated orchestra of divers who conjured deeper and deeper descents into now-submerged irrigation tracts and channels.

Even before the deluge and the theatrical attempts at rescue there had already been enacted an anticipation by flight. Elizabeth-Eberhardt was the agronomist in our team of cultural survey and was the last to join us at Manchester village. Elizabeth-Eberhardt was an Amerindian whose parents had died of malnutrition when she was a girl. She had been fostered and sent to the Catholic Mission in Georgetown. She was schooled, won a scholarship, and at university studied the plantation of the Interior – an ironic reflex to save in retrospect the generation before her who starved and died. Elizabeth-Eberhardt flew to join us from her research post in Trinidad. Thus unwittingly, like her Carib ancestors a thousand years before her, Elizabeth-Eberhardt continued to invade and re-invade the Guianas from the Caribbean islands.

As an agronomist studying the migratory garden spaces of the indigenous tribes, Elizabeth had, in a sense, built her career with the Amerindians in the North West district. She made famous rallies into the interior, sometimes touching down, it was reported, in the narrow lanes of white sand that bordered cataracts and clearings in the dense jungle. It seems to me that in the particular territory of imagination she occupied in the team, Elizabeth-Eberhardt is identified with the rainbow-serpent whose body is believed, by those peoples of the North African deserts who hold onto vestiges of pre-Islamic cosmology, to be the material of the world. Thus Elizabeth-Eberhardt's flying glasses were prismatic with the rainbow. There was a connection, too, between the Tudor rose she wore embroidered on a silken neckerchief and the English Virgin Queen – though it was widely rumoured in the fertile ribbon of the Guyana rivers that Elizabeth had borne a child of melded ancestry; a love-child angel whose fact of being may have become entangled in my own restitution.

On her first arrival, the whole of Manchester village assembled to watch Elizabeth land. We waved her down from her aerial canoe of conquest; we watched her bring to land her prop-plane, the hull shored upward.

Conquerless ships, harbourless arks, relocated cities, Celts, Hollanders, Cayennes, British, native peoples: my musings concerning them generated conspiratorial time in the annual masquerades and made me reach for a multitude of masks – the macaw-mask for stalking Death; the dove-mask for counterfeigning Love; the pelt of the three-toed sloth to don against a certain inconsistent anatomy in the hornblower's valveless throat. In their bridle-less passions I became a human marker in a swaying memory compass that for a period slipped time's magnetism.

Elizabeth-Eberhardt landed on the strip of coast, climbed down from the wires and kite-frame of the cockpit and crossed the East Coast road into Manchester village. The Hindu children were the first to catch up with her, for their village was on the immediate lea of where she landed. As she crossed the East Coast Road into the village, the sinewed sons and lissom daughters of Brahma and their Hindi tongues swarmed about her hot and red like marabuntas accompanying a fat-hoard back to the love nest. The children of African descent also came out to her, but one by one. They were shy like fruit bats lured into the blinding glare of the sun. One by one they came out with their furry heads and intermittent piping voices that tweaked at the orienting of time and tide, then shied away again as the clocks switched and unsettled time.

Laban, rude, bare-torsed and single-lunged (he had lost one to infant pleurisy) had come out of the Hall of Fame (the Manchester School House which the ethnographic team occupied). He had walked the brief length of the main street and planted his conqueror's foot on the pediment of the bridge-dam that spanned the flood catchment between the East Coast road and the village.

Elizabeth-Eberhardt was already crossing the bridge toward Laban without becoming aware of him. She had already removed her air helmet, her goggles, wiped her forearm across her brow and squinted to her right at the collapsing wings of the sun. Elizabeth! Elizabeth! Touched by so many children. Their hands are blithe with time. How carelessly touch and its spillage of hope, like invisible rainfall, returns time and again to indiscernible water-catchments.

When the deluge came Elizabeth had been fumbling for something dropped in the cockpit of the moon, whose horns and buttresses had began to uncrown or efface themselves, remaining visible solely to occult perception.

Laban leaned into the stirrup of the bridge-dam to attract Elizabeth's attention, but she was already scrutinising the fosse below the dam, momentarily holding her goggles to her face again, like a swimmer or plunger rehearsing a point of entry. The children were pointing at the places where her gaze flashed.

Had the flood-catchment held water when a Fairmaid dancer had captured the young soul of Elizabeth-Eberhardt, as she had once told me?

"No," Elizabeth replied, as if overhearing me from my position at Laban's shoulder. "No, Leon-Battista. It was in the backdam behind the village that I saw the Fairmaid on my way home from the rice farms."

I could see that in the creatured labyrinth of the daytime moon, Elizabeth-Eberhardt was rehearsing in her mind the Fairmaid's undulating dance. Intercourse with the past is a slow attractor of trust in sightings that are veiled and indeterminate, but Elizabeth and her Fairmaid had surrendered themselves.

"The Fairmaid and her reckless rivermaid dance pitched a fever in my susceptible body," Elizabeth had once said to me when we lay side by side in our hammock of love. Since the day she encountered the Fairmaid – some fifteen years before her current arrival in the Carib ship of conquest – there had been living in Elizabeth a kind of consumption that was a burning in her flesh and a burning-out of her life. Elizabeth, the aerial virgin in a cloth of a

41

thousand daylight stars, announced in her arrival our ready-made picture of a romantic life. The intense conflagration in her residual flesh was the perishable fuel for the desire and longing she engendered in me. In the glare of the sun, her violet-coloured eyes seemed to declare the still-being-mapped constellations of the austral sky hidden in daylight. Her skin was both dusk and fair. It gave the impression of eventide's permanent approach; encroaching and forever postponed; like the approach of a horn to a trumpeter's lips, a horn capsized with messaging music that would fluster the skin in increasingly complex tones; tones that expose the fallacy of race or one's own collapse at the mouth of a Jericho trumpet announcing a day whose end is continually deferred. Fearing that collapse made me stand still in Elizabeth's Long Day.

"Were you not terrified, Elizabeth, by the extrusion of the unsuspected and the covert made suddenly apparent in your conventional sphere?"

"Because the fosse was empty, Leon-Battista, I heard the Fairmaid with great clarity when she whispered my name. It was evening. I had been working on the rice farms. I was crossing the backdam home when she spoke with me. Why I pause here on the front-dam is because I am glimpsing on this mounted spur of a bridge not the actual place of the event, but seeing again the sudden and precipitous families of resemblance that bear us in hybrid yet legitimate kinship with species of being other than those we recognise to be our own."

My glance flicked back to Laban as Elizabeth said this. The forked hairs of his bare neck and shoulder were coarse and tawny. Around and beneath a sleeveless vest Laban wore public hair as the devil would wear a red-hair coat, persistently and with aberrant disregard for climate or hour of day. I was valet to the devil in his commodious abyss. I brushed his frock-coat, the thread made unruly by the tug of supergravity. I dried the mercurial broken strings of hydragyrum from the cloth-skin hat cut from the pelt of a tapir while ministering to the hallucination of quantum gravity in which we displaced ourselves. I was a dry-water/wetland candidate for anomaly and its vanishing cosmogonic constant: the constant of psyche and cosmos.

Laban had stood in the crook of fame and stretched his crozier to his flock. He had collared us one by one and put us to the side two by two. This was in the ark of the school house. Elizabeth had been with us a fortnight when he touched her neckerchief with the rim of his crook in a curious nestling gesture, as if not to disturb it unduly. The petals of the white Tudor rose were picked-out in bright strings by the whitening bone of the crozier, which tilted like a disbursed crown in the flower. There was a startling of the air when the assembly saw this.

What curious franchise! Laban's gesture was not solely a grotesque re-enactment of collaring us into his fold. Beneath Laban's kindling gesture, if only for a moment, we all flowered briefly with the fragrance of roses and attar. That swift and vanishing translation we all remembered.

Elizabeth put her hands together.

You are cast out when you do not accept unhesitatingly the articles of continual abdication that sponsor how to think, feel, treat one another and be creative in ways conforming to the perceived naturalism in human nature. To swerve from the naturalism of the human exposes you to elements others cannot afford. The modernism of disappearance. Afraid for themselves, others push you out as they would push a scout into uncharted wilderness but do not speak of you as a pathfinder, but label you a wilful renegade. I became a *swerver* or trader with the hinterland and its parable of being in a larger unseen composition, while lacking everything of Laban's mastery of masks. In this respect, as the following episode amply illustrates, I carried still a native naivety.

One day we were gathering data on the masquerade figures in preparation for filming the celebration, and we fell into a technical discussion on nativeness and civilization.

"What exactly is culture, Leon-Battista?" Laban laughed. He puckered his lips about these words as if he were a trombonist preparing to spit in the mouthpiece before committing himself to blow.

"We take fractions of things and make them stand for the whole; fractions of custom, fractions of practice, fractions of ways of doing things we find familiar and we make them stand for culture. We are fertile with fractions," I replied.

Laban spat, shook his crozier, *alaurmed* his death rattle. As if to ward off Laban's crook of death, I opened my covenant box and took out its instruments: an electronic notebook; an audiovisual recorder whose optic wand swung outward like an aileron or solo wing into a silent screen. On that screen I framed the team. I drafted cathode-ray cartoons of Forbes, Alicia, Elizabeth, Melville and Laban, first outlined in micro-point before their translation into realism; their bleeding into technical colour.

It was then I saw the ghost-angels, fore-images, in the corners of the lens. Their bodies and trumpets elongated uppermost and always just within the picture frame to uphold an hierarchy of pictorial space in the formal composition. How well I knew that strain!

"For God's sake, put that thing away, Modaal. How can we hear ourselves think!"

I dimmed the apparatus and the flair of the angels' trumpets dimmed. Had Laban heard it too?

"We should outline," I began, "the conquistadorial ground of pageant in the Guianas."

We were standing in an abandoned garden space in the lands behind the brick-dam of Manchester village. At one time the clearing would have been planted by Amerindians who would move on then return short weeks later to collect the harvest. Now the clearing was a wild-garden, an open ambulatory for the moon.

"Native imagination, it seems to me, can be thought of as one in which there is a capture of discontinuous and anachronistic time, locale and, seemingly, of events."

Laban countered, "Those are words from an angel's mouthpiece, Leon-Battista. A storm comes and the moon descends to our irrigation dyke and draws tide at the water-gate. I have a role in this carnival, this parade of flesh, that may consume you."

I had been warned. I held my breath, a constraining spirit-line with which to measure the cascade from Forbes, Alicia, Melville. Those lines puckered, made flux about Elizabeth.

"To the straightforward eye," I insisted, "events appear improvised, provisional, and hybrid. The comprehensive writing of history, it seems to me, should take into continual account, the endemic hybridity at the heart of the culture. Such a history would be a constant reading through instances, such as the twinning of Lancaster, Liverpool, and Manchester on different continents; not to be read as providential symmetry, but as the mixing and melding that inform belief, bias, and action within the fluid identity that constitutes the culture."

Laban made the sign of the splintered cross; a jagged, deceiving gesture with the hand and the doubting thumb. He kissed that thumb on its knuckle bone. It was then I knew that I had thrown in my lot with an archdevil and had unwittingly begun the mummering of monstrous runes in his deforming crozier, which was as much hellfire raiser as magus-wand.

My first complete view of the timehr took place far in the future. Time had shoved me in an unwitting periscope that sighted the year two thousand and two and cast a backward shadow on the body of the young boy discovered run-down on the coastal road of a revisited, prediluvian Manchester village in the days leading up to the cataclysm.

In April of that future year, with a feeling of strange unease, I had risen from my future memory bed and rested my feet in a thicket of coarse grass to steady myself. I heard a faint but distinct murmur, like the drafts of warm noontime air that precede the afternoon rain. I could not quite stand up. Something doubled me over; cut me in half. The pliant wind met, then separated, the stalks of grass. A terrible and invisible hand flung the timehr, thirsty and broken, into the long grass.

His berry-brown child's body was painted in plantain green with vermillion hoops. A macaw's scarlet tail was affixed to his head like the relocated staff of an exhausted herald, and indeed his arms and legs shook and that violent shaking seemed to pin his head directly to the ground.

"Do not be horrified," he sighed. "It is an earth tremor breaking the sea bed fifty miles offshore and borrowing my body as an experimental quake organ."

He smiled through a fissure close to his mouth, a fissure, I suddenly noticed, remarkable in that it resembled the colour and stagger of the red ochre stain I remember seeing on Laban's mouth on what I now began to guess had been the afternoon a small boy was reported struck down on the East coast road outside Manchester village.

I clasped my hands in a laving gesture and it came to me that Laban might have washed down the impact and its stain from the paintwork of his Bedford truck, and that the stain, fearing oblivion, might have leaped from the truck to score his chin and throat.

"You are protecting Laban, even though he is long dead," I pleaded to the painted child. "He killed you on the road, did he not? He was drunk at midday."

The fissure next to the timehr's mouth partly healed over in what may have been a glimpse of history's true complexion – seeking to flesh out and conserve at the expense of the unpalatable. If the timehr was prepared to omit unwholesome truth, to jest at truth's expense, did that not imperil me?

"Timehr," I cried, desperately, in that future year two thousand and two, "let me offer you a pact. Since you are broken and dismembered, let me loan you my own body in what I admit may only be a temporary arrangement. Borrow the life in my body and use it to revision the doubtful grounds of manslaughter. For it was manslaughter, was it not, and Laban hid his crime?"

Timehr had begun to weep. Tears brimmed at the fissure next to his mouth. Tears washed the face of the timehr's spirit body.

"Is it not strange, Leon-Battista, that the spirit can be killed as readily as the flesh, and that it should be the flesh that does the killing?"

When I returned to Manchester village and my contest with Laban in nineteen eighty-four I knew nothing as yet of his criminal act. I had only the premonition of trials, of the life of a variety of masks even as I grasped a burning bush. In my argument with Laban, I was like a new evolutionist who was secretly and carefully regrafting the flammable texts of history and cultural institution that had been fire-branded with natural selection.

I was certain that in this new turning of buried and manifest fact I myself would not be selected for natural continuance! I was going against Laban and, in the new modernism of disappearance, the elements we wrestled in – the continuous or sequential historic line, the causal world, our coercion into determinist or manifest outcome – are inimical to life, and that is undoubtedly part of their indelible fascination, our fascinated courtship with extinction.

Jacob-Israel Laban stood in the ark of righteousness and judgement, his name resurfacing again in our times as an archaeology of the patriarch who does not die, but goes to incubate in the mountains until the temptation to naturalism in human nature – the continual abdication from our comprehensive selves – sponsors him once more into cultural institution. I had hoped that some argument or persuasion or entreaty on my part could move him from his monolith stance, and for some days cast about for words that would bring home to him that such stances, symmetries, ingrained ways of framing, of moulding tired old anatomies onto our living skeleton would precipitate our whole extinction.

I knew that if I was still Laban's creature, then the words I cast for and netted would be hopelessly famished and thin. He would not have considered them. I made no mention of my premonitionry glimpses of the timehr in two thousand and two, even though his presence would have been foremost in my future memory. I did not mention to Laban that I could remember the future with the same facility that one could forget the past.

I became Laban's covert enemy. Enemy of the heart. We began to swerve and avoid one another. The whites of our eyes flashed but our gazes ceased to meet. How swiftly came the loss of mutual regard. In our own secret ways we also began to contest for the female aviator. Who would win her?

Laban had disembarked as the native son, come home to Guyana as conqueror, technologist and father of a new human commonwealth. This new study, funded by a global bank of economic harmonisation, demanded that a figure as prominent as Laban be appointed to head the study. In his very selection, Laban was part of the funder's agenda.

That question of agenda, of things to be done, had re-awoken in me in the new-visage year of two thousand and two. Above my memory bed of the future and the painted child's splintered cradle of bones, the moon was crescented and gave to the sky an amber dusk illumination against which I glimpsed a frame kite that wore a mask of feathers. I knew it was a kite because it flew on a vibrating quantum string that hummed and stretched upward barely visible from a guiding hand I did not yet recognize. I knew it was a mask because when I peered up in the evening sky I could see a semicircular bow of reeds curved in the shape of a face whose radiant hair was composed of blue plumes, and whose features were arranged in quadrants of ochre (feathers of a numinous owl), and the mouth was a horizontal bar of pitch bitumen, the tongue a dangling matchstick affixed by a string, the nose a lump of white clay fixed to the pitch, and the eyes, refractive bands of white shell.

Pitched forward to that future, I sensed that the timehr was beginning to accept my offer. I was able to isolate his presence within myself and feel its downy edges. That presence threw a rudimentary archway of things inexplicably recalled behind a membrane of cold fire. The timehr was a guest of divergent origin in my future body of oblivion, an immaterial child who sought to understand its birth.

The mask on the kite seemed to me like the facade worn by prisons. Through its eye-slits I had the unnerving feeling of a reclusive chamber whose dimensions were continuous with the night. Yes. Night was not itself a prison but a singular chamber continued by the mask. In seeking to see behind the mask I felt I would be sourcing an origin in the dimensions of an illuminated calendar, and the question occurred to me as to whether there was a correlation between self-adjusting structures and the sources that fed them.

The kite dipped suddenly and set the sky reeling. I now saw it wore a tail of satin fire that stabbed to the right and left like the barbs of a manta ray.

To my mind's eye, it sought to outline a jagged archway of cold flame at the same time as it was attempting to adjust the way of framing the world.

I felt strongly the threat of framing strategies that endanger biosystems. Each time I looked at a conventional painting of the landscape I had sensed a hollowness at the heart of the picture: trees, waters, mountains, skies: all squeezed inside an oblong shaped to human perspective. Now I realised that few painters or poets have thought to ask: what is the tree's perspective of the forest, the perspective of mountains from the Earth mantle, the river's perspective of its watersheds, and the spheres' perspective of the heavens? Would there not be a unique vision to each of these natural lives? Do we not owe it to ourselves to find the rhythms and music and language of each of these extra-human lives? Otherwise do we not continue to paint a same portrait over and over again as if a piece of our brain were damaged? Is this not oblivion, and does such rigidness, fixity, not injure nature, endanger us?

There was a breathlessness, a palsy which accompanied the insight. As if upon a humid membrane I felt a canny, mystic nativity unfold in the shocks sent out by the ocean-quake before the tidal wave came to land. The team routinely carried a seismograph in regions where it was beginning to be suspected that climatic adverses had shaped prehistory; but at Manchester village we were more encumbered by the sudden drops in humidity and I remember the sloping spidery scrawl on the diurnal drums of graph paper and how Laban mounted these on the display board as if they were a priceless archaeological resource.

"We are living in a punctured lung, Leon-Battista," I remember him saying. "The membrane is drying out yet we continue to frame our response in terms of the air's saturation with water. Is it not perverse?"

"Laban," I hesitated. "Should we not be looking for a hidden nativity among the heralds of the masquerade? The long lady and the donkey man and the whistling man and the rice doll, have we not happened upon their gestures midway in a larger unseen composition?"

Laban, I remember, had stared at me; and in the scope of two thousand and two, the stare appeared baneful and rimmed in stone. Laban's gaze brought me face to face with what I did not suspect: Laban knew all along, yet continued regardless. Slave to habit and habitual ways of responding to the world, Laban had chosen not to free himself of habit; he had consciously chosen to remain in the habitual frame of the world. Laban was where he was by choice, and not, like me, in the torment of exeat. Our difference was so blatant, so obvious, that it had not occurred to me. In opposing Laban, had I myself exercised such admirable freedom of choice? If not, to what avail my effort?

I drew breath once more and eased myself back to the wet meadow of submerged Manchester village. My weeping lung climbed a herald's memory tree as a lookout. From his herald's nest, the angel of the weeping lung begun a cribbing, cradling song, an unexpected ventriloquism with identity.

"At twilight today I flew over the capital city of Georgetown," the lung sang to me. "There are children there, in Sophia, in Brickdam, in Kitty, who live in the street. Yes, in the very street. The street is their true home. They are not dispossessed, they are not runways, they are not abandoned – although neglect was their first nativity, their primary cradle – they are simply street children, like there are house children and town children and country children; they are street children."

"What can I do?" I asked the lung.

"There is nothing you can individually do, Leon-Battista. You are always looking to act, to do oft as you think it." The lung-song broke off, then continued as if gathering momentum, "The World

Bank's need to establish indices of poverty pushes to the fore certain unquestioned premises which, as self-evident agendas, steer proceedings."

I began to reflect on what the lung told me while he borrowed the moon's ambulatory to go out from me. With the lung-song gone, I subsided once more, wholly among my peers.

I thought about Laban. There was something in him that would not give, that would not yield consciously at some level; his seemed to me a wilderness declaration. I, formerly his main-man, Thomas-Thumb or prehensile grip on our contract with one another, had secretly broken seal, had become Devil's advocate, begun to question myself and my civilisation.

It seems to me that the habit of continual abdication from one's counter-intuitions might contribute to the fallacy of perceived naturalism in human nature. I myself practised expedience, abdicated continually to that fallacy if only to win the space that would further my own ends. Expedience furthers continuance. And because expedience always takes place at the expense of others, I began to recognise that my own continuance became a distancing from others. Victim of territorial constraint, I felt the need to act on the sly if I was to win gross-room for myself. The displacements of my sleeping, singing self required greater intervals or expressions of scale than that in which I was living. Like many others I hid from myself the self-administered famine that kept me secretly needy and undependable.

What I suffered!

When Laban began to pontoon the small handful of rice boats together – the little flatpan barges on which harvested rice was floated-in from the backfarms to the rice sheds – he seemed to stoop and whistle and tilt and tie with the same inflections as Elizabeth when she had pre-enacted for the whole village the dance of the Fairmaid.

Was it Elizabeth's dance that had sparked off in Laban's head the association with deluge and flood? In a way, the whole village caught on to the paradiluvian connection. In her Fairmaid dance, Elizabeth seemed to float upright on the backdam with blunted head and snout and paddle-shaped forelimbs, her lower limbs bound together like a courtesan's, so that below the bindings it seemed to fan and splay. Her animal yet human crossmorphery was accentuated further by the three tiny nails she showed in her forelimbs, nails that seemed to be encrusted with small diamonds that glittered as though they were the point-sources of the evening. I expect it was her love of disguise, the need to sustain indeterminacy, which recommended to Elizabeth's dramatic senses the cascading dusk as the time for trial and re-enactment. From a distance the children mistook her for a sea-cow or manatee which had caused the water suddenly to rise above the dam and had made us spectators of a submerged though apparent spectacle.

From the dam's causeway the children thrilled and shrieked. Beads of perspiration broke like fine milk on the brow of the larger women. Some of the men sucked at their teeth partly in distress, partly in manifold suckling.

Elizabeth enacted the anomalous or the taxonomic inconstancy of a mammal that has no kinship with the whales yet which also lives its entire life in water. In retrospect I feel that her human-manatee-Fairmaid cross-habitation caused a secret displacement in all of us, so that without knowing it we were already turning our dusk-lit fronts to what in the unencumbered light of day would have seemed inadmissible. The clarity of Elizabeth's movements slipped further into night. They grew cavernous and began to swallow the participants in her dance.

It is said that the silhouette of the manatee is duplicator of the many stories of Fairmaids that branch from the rivers and estuaries of the Everglades, the Caribbean, the northern and eastern coasts of South America and West Africa. In China the surrogate mammal or wet-maid is the river dolphin. In the brine of the Red Sea, the Indian Ocean and off Australia it is the dugong. No such creatures exist in European waters yet the legend is in Europe too.

What could account for Europe's anomaly? Did the Gulf Stream deliver messages from the deltas of South America to Europe's shores that Europe's men of prehistory, upon the seas and in the river mouths, could discern? Has that message since become permanently jammed in the loop of con-

vention so that we have emptied Europe's rivers –
as if by removing all the fish the rivermaids would
surface again? Thus I remember myself being especially attentive for instances of jamming or premature closure in Elizabeth's Fairmaid dance.

By being attentive to the one especial thing, we
are sometimes able to attend to the imminent part
of ourselves that has awaited only for the right
means and capacity for expression in some forever
postponed and unparalleled performance.

Laban's cutlasses are examples of instruments *en*
attentent from a vanished or as yet to be realised
performance. They had twitched in anticipation of
capacity. He had used them to cut the hemp-rope
moorings of the pontoon as well as to defend the
ark. A finger, a hand, sometimes a larger portion of
anatomy that did not figure in *his* natural selection
or species for continuance would be judged and fall
beneath the blade. He deployed his sentences as
though he feared being trapped by them. Within a
given judgement he veered widely from his own
previous counsel as from some constraining influence until, at last satisfied by the pleaders's confusion, he would have them kiss him before turning
them finally away. In the guise of the fateful kiss,
followed by dismissal, everyone became Laban's
accomplices in self-betrayal – an indeterminate con-
gregation of blind inner hearing and a compulsive
yet intermittent seeing. Laban's was a cruel – and I
now believe emancipating – cut that robbed us of
sensation. Deprived of direct perception through

the traditional five senses, we had until then no notion of how to read messages which were of a non-sensational nature and which passed unnoticed or smothered by the sensational world. I will come back to this later since the capacity to read our non-sensational nature is crucial to these times and offers, it seems to me, conscious exit from extinction.

Laban's quiet rebukes confused us. Their very quietness subdued us so that we were not as agile as we might have been, but submissive and fatefully accepting. It was with that instrument, I believe, that Laban struck down Elizabeth on the ark. O hand of passion! O instrument of passion in psychical hands! Laban struck her with his passionate hands and Elizabeth collapsed below the crozier.

She joined her hands together on her knees. The cloud of the ark veiled them. Those hands that Laban in extreme passion intended to sever, those hands, I believe, secretly etched runes in the wood of the ark's capstan to which Laban would tie her.

Part of my own weakness is my incompetence with physical violence. I had matured into half a man who did not know how to prevail in the depredations of shock and danger. I was not so much a coward as thoroughly ineffectual. This was my leprosy. It made me lazarine and barely fit for continuance.

Laban came to stoop in the ark of selfhood. He had bound Elizabeth's hands to a capstan and rested the cutlasses on her naked wrists. I lay concussed, partly on the deck, partly overboard, weeping with the wound in my head, a paralysed posture that partly boarded, partly abandoned the pontoon. I lay dreaming the fall of the cutlass and the release of Elizabeth's hands from their prayerful bondage.

Just as Laban's unbridled judgement showed catastrophic schism with whole-world or non-sensational realities, just so did our own subsidence in the face of his acts constitute an equally premature closure with fate; for capitulation is intrinsic to rehearsed changes in sensibility: I had followed Laban's unbridled judgment as if he were my prompter, and I performed his musics of realism from a musician's crib. That crib was a rocking, mendacious song, a liar's cradle song for a troubling infant, virgin mother and surrogate father. I rocked my crib of capitulation with maiden hands in a chamber of annunciation.

I was to board two arks, virtual arks, virtual oceans, virtual harbours. I trembled on a slippery walkway hoping not to make snap judgements about the kind of ship I was entering.

We negotiated with illusory notions that were no more than the diseased fruit of a liberal tradition. Our pathetic arguments turned about justifications concerning free will, individual freedom and natural selectivity. I should state that we never said these things aloud. We were too numbed with anticipation. It was when we wedged ourselves in tiny fissures of time that we most sought to observe our study as one would observe a discrete system, remotely and with detachment. It was chiefly then,

I am sure, that we abdicated and made ourselves contingent with justification.

Hours before the police came, a Hindu woman holding a bundle of rice plants had knocked on the door of the mission school. Alicia answered and chose cadences in her voice that would deflect the woman's enquiry. She embraced the bereft mother whose voice had broken and given way to low catastrophic booms in the interior of the school room. Such was the measure of Laban's confidence in his own power that he did not trouble even to look up. I begin to wonder if his arrogation did not also factor a continued, implicit trust in me. Did he believe I would climb into the ark with him?

But the walkway to the ark was berthed on a margin of common land I did not recognise my own right to. It was this that foxed me. My new unknowing. In my new unknowing, the walkway was laid in planks of purpleheart that were at once a bridge to the virtual arks, at once weeping with splinters from a capitulated rood reappearing miraculously in our time in Manchester village.

A line of conduct was needed; a firm but subtle lifeline that could survive the determinism of linear history; that passage from acts to consequences, that culture of causality that took no account of the discontinuity in consciousness that was to be enforced by my loss of memory.

My own non-sensational reality, my timehr, came to me in my gutted ark of memory.

"Was it about that time, Leon-Battista, as you began to wage secret war and rebellion against Laban, that you began to construct theorems of the world's geomancies; the geomancy of origin and extinction: contemporary Iraq superimposed above the cradle and possible future grave of civilisation?"

I nodded at the timehr's presence.

"First occurring to me was the geomancy of brute mutilation: central African republics where administrative boundaries cut into the flesh of distinct peoples and dismembered them from traditional homelands.

"Geomancy of rejected blood-mix: central American and Caribbean Hispanic republics (Hispanic Caribbean identity) that despise the African legacy betrayed in the sallow skin of the whitest circum-Caribbean individuals and in languages such as the Palenquero of Colombia and Panama, the Papiamento of Aruba and the Garifuna of Yurumei-St. Vincent. In these languages we are confronted with a strange Heisenbergian density through which to reassess our dominant interpretation of natural selectivity. In the first two languages we can readily identify the indigenous, European, then African donations to Caribbean Spanish; but it is in Garifuna that we confront the most extraordinary instance of institution or absolutely-conserved phenomena. Although the vocabulary of Garifuna carries no trace of African words – it is chiefly remnant of indigenous Arawak and Carib with European syncretions – the phonetics of the language, its sounds, intervals, intonations, are entirely African, as if the shipwrecked transportees of the sixteen-fifties divined to conceal not only their corporeal goods from recapture, but also to hide their presence in language behind the blind of hearing. *Akoumancy* or survival-institution by way of inner audition."

The timehr stood immobile as if to quit his *hacienda celesti*, as if by this attitude he would avoid attracting special attention to himself. Now he asked me.

"So in what way, for you, Leon-Battista, does Guyana constitute a new contemporary society that describes and continues the geomancies that seem to have accumulated so steeply in our age?"

"Guyana and the Guianas and the wider South and Central American continent encompass fulgurance. Fulgurance of blood-mix, fulgurance of art, fulgurance of a technology of the imagination, fulgurance of teleology or suspended pacts with design: suspension of evolutionary design, historical design, political design..."

My voice tailed off and I continued to myself: none of those indices, so well accounted for in reckonings of the West, have established a constant footing or metric base in the Americas, so that Guyana, unbound from design, is free in a sense to prospect with the future. It did not enter our heads that we were also dramatising a parable of temporal indeterminacy in which our current acts altered events in the far past, and the motives in an as yet unperceived event can so transpose us that we are permanently precipitated in an as yet to be recognised future. It went unnoticed by us, this community with our unborn selves we divined in Guyana.

The Guyana coastland – its monotony, its suffocated breath-lines – exerts a flattening of certain historical dimensions. The rescue and resuscitation of a lost perspective from the burying landscape might repopulate a stage better able to accommodate a drama encompassing a broken symmetry, a broken chronology, the symbols of brokenness occurring to us when the structures we adhere to are too rigid, when they cannot accommodate our community with all living things. Rigidness breaks itself in order to allow a new fluid identity. Symmetries in our thought and conceptions of ourselves clog up the blood vessels in the body of civilisation.

The survey team – which I now see was made up of hapless synchronists or failed jugglers of sequential time – willed for itself, just as did the Dutch in the sixteen hundreds, the coastal strip of Guyana as the site to cull and mark in a prologue to bring us name and fortune. We cinched with the coastal belt of Guyana, we nested and bred in the mud-girdle – which is not just the alluvial deposit of river systems, but also a fertile crescent able to nourish an august parable. We noted how the crescent is also the horn of the moon and the pregnant cornucopia of populations and states. Such populations (Carib, Columbian, colonial, contemporary) continue to congregate in the formal shaped horn of the South America continent to hear the reading when the advocates of the living emerge from the night bush and begin, finally, to pronounce from the antediluvian futuring book of being. It was with some intimation of this, I believe, that the world's geomancies began to occur to me for, later, as I was to lie weeping in the pleurisy of the mud-lung, evading rescue and its inevitable reducing of myself into history's zealous determinism (Leon-Battista came here, did this, said this, had this happen to him), it was with the sense of a prediluvian reading that I stammered in and out of sleep.

Was this one of the readings tattooed in the skin of Amalivacar, the great advocate of the Guianas? Was it for him I was waiting, crying into my sleep so that he would hear me more clearly and perhaps increase his speed?

I remember a moment when my inner seeing ear sought him in the night bush and I began to pronounce the epigraphs written in his skin, to decipher them with my dreaming tongue. My tongue became fleet with dreaming and able for a moment to bear a full burden of aesthetic meaning. Its range extended. My dreaming tongue itself became a soma or epigraphic body among the many others thronging Amalivacar's skin. Its expression was powerful enough to compel from me meditations on advocacy and judgement.

Amalivacar is the Amerindian god of art and for me an advocate for life's continuity in the Guianas.

We communicate intuitions by expressing them in artistic form. We undertake these communications without absolute claim. Being of this world they partake of the same nature as the world. A man who has lost his memory is left with gaps in a continuous lifeline. His personal history develops a hole that will abhor its sense of void. Cultures also suffer from amnesia; technologies known to prior ages are lost, only to be rediscovered later and in other places. Imaginative traditions disappear, only to be resurrected in surprising and unrelated arts. It is the unstated purpose of history to fill or, rather, conceal these holes. Few chroniclers will have the humility to leave blanks for what is not known, and the courage to signal that this is so.

When an individual suffers discontinuities of time – the loss of memory failing to interrupt the passage of events, a cultural loss of memory making blank and invisible holes in the continuous historical line – he is obliged to read from another source if he is to fill-out the anomaly in his account, if in the remnants he is to arrive at some perspective. Unable to affirm or deny events taking place during memory's bankruptcy, his is a current account without currency. Liquidity, fluidity, then, become the medium of acceptance that can include the forgotten, the it-escapes-us memory.

"Timehr," I cried in sudden, stricken terror. "What if the community with our discontinuing selves continues to elude human history? What if no testament with time can be arrived at that will create a passage between a yet-to-be apprehended past and a reappraised future: is my conscience without foundation?"

A bell rang in the future, as cracked as the earth's crust, yet sound. It seemed to be suspended in the recessive chamber of the mask-kite as a kind of declaration with time that would prolong the self through a void.

It was then that the naked design of dreaming came home to me. Amalivacar carried a book of paradoxical pericopes written in the glyphs on his skin. What if the language of Amalivacar's skin glyphs should relate to the language of dream and put forward hypotheses that bear on changes in human nature that may be non-sensational; ones we may not be able to perceive with our five senses but ones whose recognition is of crucial importance for our future as a species? My eyes swung back to the rice-boat and to Laban.

"You are missing the obvious, the blatant, Leon-Battista," Laban exulted, "The very strength of sensation is its own law. It is independent of jurisdiction." He did not trouble to raise his cutlasses to make his point. I was no threat to him where I lay.

"The wound in my head begs to differ, Laban. It is saying, 'What if the dream is a maker of hypotheses concerning the parable of man and that that parable is one that requires special fictions whose material is as often as not the stuff of vanishing traditions?'"

Laban paused. Elizabeth turned from him. Strange rain began to drizzle, a veil holding both cloud and antimony. I had forgotten. Laban never dreamed. He had told me that he had never had a dream. He hated dreams at the same time as failing to comprehend how dreams had been ambushing him into life. It did not occur to him that the way they eluded his waking memory, the way they stalked him with half-numb memories of memories, the way they kept on substituting objects of mentation for real imaginative elan, kept him unconceived, as one who is constantly impregnated but never falls pregnant; a man of ghost pregnancies that relentlessly approach but do not apprehend term.

Elizabeth's eyes held dreamscape. They let flow milligrams of water that suddenly clarified, like a droplet in a sealed glass phial. It was in this *camera lucida* that I glimpsed an opening.

"The wound in his head begs, Laban," Elizabeth said.

This unsettled Laban, as if he had dropped in an air pocket. He fought for breath as one fights to regain altitude.

"The begging wound draws up ichor from the tumid ground. It pumps and gushes with a glassy action. A seal is put on it, but mercy might break the seal just as an ambush will beset our best precautions on the road of conversion and self-forgiveness."

What a reversal! What blinding of a cherished line of sight. My arm grew numb with zig-zag lines. It was almost pulled out with shock lines. Little had prepared me for Laban's merciless conversion of an habitual ventriloquism of voice into an uncanny organ of spiritual speech. I turned my head to confound him, to show him the wound he had cut in it with the ventriloquist's unforgiving blade; but the wound refused to show itself to Laban. It refused to size him. The wound had more knowledge than it imparted and was reserving that knowledge for a future date.

In April two thousand and two, doubled over on my memory bed, the mask-kite and its future recessive chamber began to sketch within itself a more expanded composition. The mask's lines of sight drew breath and began to draw with breath. They ran outward to nineteen eighty-four to model and clothe my body (whether by soft shadow or tensile strength) in such a way that the positions of my arms and legs become expressions of the emotions remaking me. My legs were drawn up under me. They implied a possibility of movement, as did my bunched shoulders and sunken head. What I needed was the illusion of space in which actually to move.

On the raft, I lay in need of accommodation in which to set the gathering lines of my body. Laban chose that moment to fall back into frame, into the round picture and geometric enclosure in which he, Elizabeth and I were temporarily arranged. The line from the tip of his extended foot joined my own hip and I toppled into the canal. Elizabeth swayed at her bonds and shook the contours of her shoulders. Was she racked with laughter? Was she drunk with mirth? Was Elizabeth-Eberhardt with her swollen belly (was it my seed, was it Laban's, was it our future child who intercepted me six years later on New Year's Day nineteen hundred and ninety-one in the market place at Linden-Macken-zie?) laughing because she saw an inevitable exit from the diabolical symmetry that had enslaved us as a team chained to one another as gang and chained gang? It is something I would never ascertain. I shared my long day with you, Elizabeth. You were, I feel dimly at this stage, a flying-over or augured passover time for me of the riddle of the marking hand; a timehri art that expresses the paradox of recuperating the perishable in the most disarming spaces: petroglyphs in the rain forest interior, irreplaceable pictograms done on tree-bark as if to frighten us into the instinct for permanence; a riddle of imaginative expression, diverging at many points to indicate that the sacred falls in scattered spaces.

When the flute-band of masquerade started up on Christmas Eve nineteen-hundred and eighty-four, I was shaken awake by the flute's imprisoning lines of melody which would not relent. The melody insisted on its own unimpeachable logic. It was a harrowing music, the most harrowing music I have experienced. It raked over me with its teeth and its tine. It rehearsed and reinforced. It determined and its whole thrust was to determine me, and with me, the very basis for music. Those were terrible moments. Terrible proclamations in a continually re-iterated succession of tones that would not entertain the possibility of hollowing itself of sound. I lay in a tent of testament with Elizabeth, a tent that seemed more winding sheet than mosquito net. Elizabeth was still putting out the lanterns of the dream.

"As I am dressed, I am," she murmured in our clarifying chamber.

A threadbare lariat of light snaked from the instruments of the flute band. Swing music. The soul in the swing of music. Music swung into the hanging noose that frames the hanging judge and the hung jury.

Hooks, black with violent bile, impaled the soul's flesh in the anatomy of that music. The voice, the guitar, the flute and the steel triangle of masquerade demonstrated before our doorway. They insinuated themselves, as do all masquerades, into the house to demand their fee – sweet cakes, rice wine, rice liquor. Behind them swayed the Long Lady (Alicia Dolphin, I think, the musicologist in our team of Cultural Survey) and between her baton legs was thrust the carnivore neck of the Donkey-Man (was that not Melville, our ethnographer proper?). Forbes was the Whistling Man (was not his the soul's true terror expressed in the escape and pneumatics of air?). Through the whistling gaps in his teeth, Forbes had unwittingly and ironically bridged the band's jolting, coupling rhythms with the precise hollowing-out of sound that the festival melody was itself unable to apprehend. The band came into our lodge on the crest of triumphal overture. Occasional music for the sovereignty of Occasion, entering in the blazon of the Sun.

Now the hall of fame from which Laban had been compelled to that first incendiary encounter at the bridge-dam with Elizabeth-Eberhardt was also the place where the lynch or anatomical mob from Liverpool village had congregated. The dismembering mob intended to treat us as if our limbs were attached to an illusory body. They intended to sever us and our limbs as one might sever a man from his illusions. Mobs stand outside the hall of compelling fame whilst god-men move obscurely within.

In one sense the arrival and encampment of the ethnographic team had fostered mistrust, fear and resentment in the adjacent villages, in another sense our arrival was also being capped and recapped in different guises by the neighbouring villages, whose spokesmen vied with one another to offer the definitive interpretation of our presence there. Yet the articles of continual abdication are tenacious. That we planned a dispassionate study of the forthcoming masquerade was a possibility that did not occur to those interpreting tongues. Benign motive did not look out from *their* analyses. Thus the tongues in Liverpool village were ripe and in-flamed. They historicised us as if *we* were a colony to be subdued, then ministered to. Our very presence was read into the naturalism of the famous insect world and our acts construed as a stripping of foliage or leaves from a sacred book of psalms. We were spoken of as the devourers of a wholesome script.

It is true that our communication of our frames of reference could have stood improvement, although their insufficiency could not altogether account for the heat and press from Liverpool village. Mostly Hindus lived at Liverpool. An old woman, a former Deccan who had been indentured from the subcontinent whilst still an infant, had been preparing the dyes for the masquerade costumes. She had looked in the dye vat and prophecy had come upon her. A skinny boy overheard her intercourse with the poisonous Fates and took it to his best friend's mother who spread it to the wider circle of mothers. Liverpool succumbed to the intoxicant of fate and prediction. Liverpool lost, literally, its innocence or absence of harm. The women pestled and mortared their husbands with it in bed at night and, in the false dawn, as the men hurried behind the backdam to the rice-farms, a plot or pact with premature closure was being drawn-up. Our closure. Our premature ending. Plans were laid to make our study null; and because the contract with closure knew of us, we became closure's unwitting instruments.

For what is instrumentality but the wilful contract with outcome? When my actions become fated with determinism I become instrumental with fate, acquire a certain instrumental value that makes me suitable for the service required of me. As instrument, my limbs are heavy with inevitability and it is in this way that I become symbiotic with tragedy. Tragedy is a pact or contract with fate; and because it is predetermined, because I abdicate the free anthology of myself, that fating destroys me. In this way comes the fallacy of naturalism in the human, in this way came my evolving alongside extinction.

Liverpool village had also heard of Elizabeth-Eberhardt's manatee dance (if prehistoric Europe had heard five thousand miles away in the apogee of the Gulf Stream, how could Liverpool village, barely two and a half miles down the coast, have failed to hear?) By its consensus, its coercion of views, the villagers considered her dance to be a form of mass enslavement. They were coming with cutlasses and lanterns with, I suspect, the secret desire to free us.

That push, that altruism for our emancipation, was perhaps the covert summons served in advance on Liverpool village by advocate Amalivacar, who at that moment was preparing his passage by way of the night bush and might have wished to set preliminary hearings prior to his arrival and ensure an articulate audience. Thus I lisped in and out of the fallacy of clarification – that desire to separate what is by nature epigraphic – as one lisps in and out of occluded speech.

Is there a conception of ourselves that accepts paradox in such matters as causality, avoids privileged frames of reference and at the same time preserves our innate complexity? Attempts at clarity can obscure the most telling clues. Claims for clarity raise a sense of despair in the individual who is complex with his or her sense of diminutive yet comprehensive being. Such an individual is aware not just of the special paradoxes that anchor man to a conception of himself as a species, and hence indissolubly bound in community (community of creation, birth, socio-economy), but is aware that man's daily round is congested with furthering glimpses (the communities of ancestors, the dead, and of our unborn selves).

Our response to these furthering glimpses, our response to congestion, precipitates the fallacy of clarity. It seduces us into attempts to capture furthering glimpses once and for good in a ready digestible formula. Yet such claims are force-ripe. They distress the acute listener with a sense of *el desdichado*, of being disinherited, fallen from his true estate. What pushes our leaders and mentors into these ludicrous frames? Why do they continue to negotiate with a diction of reality that sidelines the most crucial issues?

"On that matter of clarity tell me, Leon-Battista, why does a cuckoo have no cocoon?" Laban had drawled one hot afternoon.

"The cuckoo has no need for a cocoon because he has got others to occupy their own cocoon of abdication," I had said. "It with this he dispossesses them."

Laban had growled with his bone-yellow teeth. My answer simultaneously met his approval of the fecund and disturbed him with its quick movement. He showed his teeth. They laced the cavern of his mouth as a shaman would lace jaguar-teeth on an ochre gut necklace.

"Let us suppose, Leon-Battista, that my mouth, my teeth, my gums, that the whole dental apparatus was also an abacus; that the teeth were individual counters in an aperture that admits morsels of flesh and morsels of thought without discrimination; the figures of thought, a digested food, the morsels of alimentation, a riddling speech. How many counters would give you your answer? How many teeth would you pull, Leon-Battista? You see, I have often wondered about Methuselah and his preservation of teeth, the words a man would have to mince if he lived longer than any known man."

My throat began to dilate. I began to see around the corners of Laban's jest. The ethnographic mission began to stagger and groan below a new burden.

Close to the speed of light the world looks very odd. Everything is squeezed into a tiny circular window that stays just ahead of you. Everything you have just passed, lived, digested, appears, paradoxically, ahead of you. In this way I lagged behind, even though I had already been admitted to Laban's *tondo* or circular jestery. Laban and I became compressed in a soulful intimacy that overtook us even as it preceded us into what had been. Laban's jaguar teeth were now yellow with carnivorous light, light that devoured, that established itself as an absolute, a special case in the ongoing creation of the universe. I rode the wave-front of creation at the edge of galaxies and for a moment knew the full extent of the soul's leisure.

"You are transfixed at a statutory front, Leon-Battista," Laban had called from the bulwark of the ark.

"Am I the wave-front and you the body of water?" I had gasped between swimming strokes.

Laban had peered at me as one would peer at an unascertainable object in the blind spot of a telescope.

"You should know that my life expresses the abandoning of teleology or argument from design," Laban had called with his devil-may-care air. "Let everything be wagered to the Devil. He always gives the price worth having."

I had continued swimming as though I was an intimate of the Devil's grandmother. In it lay my salvation. If one is to solve the Devil's riddles, one must speak to a familiar who is older than the Devil. One must go back to an historic layer older than the Devil that also informs the Devil. The Devil lives with his grandmother or matricelle of the culture. She is as old to him as the Sumer-Accadians are to Judeo-Christianity. We still carry the Babylonian zodiac in our popular calendar. In Central America, the descendants of the "Cloud People" still name their offspring after the Mixtec calendar which assigned to each day a name and number.

My spine has missing and collapsed numbers, curvatures that I would rather were not there, clades and spurs that articulate uneasily with one another – some askew, others slumped and slipped from an easy communion. That morning, Christmas Eve nineteen hundred and eighty-four, in an attempt to regain an upright posture, I tried to fend the band from Elizabeth and myself (I knew by then that they had come for me and that Laban had sent them) the way an animal tamer would retreat into the cage and shut the gate against the beast. I had misplaced my black revolver (blanks drawn against my abdicating self) and grappled about for something that would have the bullet's impact. The flute-band and masquerade figures burst like a sun from eclipse into our bedroom and consumed the final fires in Elizabeth's dream. Later, many light years hence, Elizabeth would show me pulsars and gamma-busters in an epoch where they would no longer be seen as abstract notations of space but might become a relocated centre of creativity. It is an imaginative resource, in our present age obscurely lodged in the host cosmologies of indigenous peoples to whom many stars and constellations are known and named in night-skyscapes that enter into their beliefs of a besides-life & death. I began to hear crochet-hooks in the deterministic yet whistling hollow of the flute-band's sound. These, to my ear, seemed to be trying to knit back together, with sound-sinews, the bursting tissue of faith in the rupture of holy communion. Forbes had torn down the rice-doll that since the harvest had been transfixed on the eaves of my house and he held her in tender embrace, a smooth, gleaning dance full of spit and polish, yet not without inti-mation of a fuller aesthetic burden.

AMALIVACAR'S EXIT FROM THE NIGHT BUSH

For women who wear nothing but their hair, the threadbare skirts of the Long Lady were an affront. She swayed eleven foot above the masquerade in a harlotry of coloured patches and a concertina of taffeta about her limp and woollen overcloth.

In the shade of the Long Lady, in her lee of skirting, Elizabeth turned to Laban a naked and brazen smile that unclothed the flesh of her mouth. On deluge day, twenty-fourth of December nineteen hundred and eighty-four, I became affixed in the smile's naked design as if caught in the traces of a cavalier horse. It tumbled me forward six years to New Year's Day, nineteen hundred and ninety-one, among the overturned stalls in Mackenzie market where I fell and recovered my memory.

The flanks of the cavalier horse were branded with the hot iron of Elizabeth's smile. Its traces were coloured in rainbow-vestments. In Mackenzie market, hawkers and traders were picking themselves up and dusting themselves down.

The reins I thought I held in my hand became, to my bolting, unblinkered eye, a picture-pageant of dreaming epigraphs that a skinny love-child had touched and placed on me as lightly as a feather. His was the gesture that bowled me over. The curve in which I fell meant that I barely caught his naked, pointed body vanishing timehri-like in the blinded corner of my eye. What if these dreaming epigraphs, *manu dei*, should be the means of signalling anomaly in our perception of causal time? What if they should permit a capillary meshing between historical layers usually perceived as separate, but which in fact might cross with one another to liberate an unsuspected community with all living things?

I fell in a capsized motion, fell out of time, cascaded in a zig-zag tempo. I called after the fleeting boy. "Timehr," I pleaded. "My own personal history has been interrupted by conquest, colonisation, assimilation, and relocation; after all that, how can I still harbour creative latencies that might bring into being a community of diverse origins?"

Timehr chuckled as he passed; I half-heard, half-intuited his reply.

"Leon-Battista Mondaal, does the survival of archaic peoples into contemporary times not offer to the intuitive imagination an opportunity to bridge a gulf between consciousness and the sense of an origin that has left no visible historical trace? What you are living, do you not meditate on it as you would a dream-parable?"

Timehr vanished. It became necessary to extend the masquerade that had taken place at Manchester not only forward to those pictograms of Amalivacar's migration, but backward too, eighteen years prior to the Manchester village masquerade and to the day when I was small and the Sun chose me for his hitching post. Such an extension is *my* reserve put on the well-tempered systems that seek to eclipse the pregnant gaps that stand aside from our expectations for formal historic coherence. The problems posed by our experience-in-time compel us to formulate ourselves in causal history, as if the symmetries of time and place were the unique solution to the problem of perception. I became the Sun's hitching post for the duration of one day, *sunday-time*. The Sun hitched itself on to me as one might hitch or establish an index within a long count. Such is the resonating chamber in which the parable of man will pitch its diffuse cloud. I seek, too, to bring the clouded chamber, in which I lay beside Elizabeth that final time, into the Manchester ark of convenation. I know that I make these epigraphic conferences of resonant spaces over time causally. It is because we lack histories of internal time-sense, ready histories that give witness to the changing beat in man's experience of the rhythms of perception, for it is precisely environments perceived as internal, where compressed air and light constellations will concentrate, that resist our best spectroscopies. In these regions human nature might undergo fundamental change without our perceiving it, just as the nature of physics might collapse and be reborn in gravitational clouds of interstellar gas and dust. Few will live in an epoch whose events literally quicken the pace of felt time without giving the character of 'fury' to intimations of the future and the sensation of destiny to the personae of the immediate past.

I am aware of a leap of stellar connections and close to the speed of light velocities. It precipitates me into the opening scenes of Manchester long before I arrived there. It rescues me, I hope, from being permanently lodged at Manchester. It makes constellations in my mind's eye so that I must almost squint to prevent them vanishing. I am stooped below that lintel of stars. I stoop with eternal gratitude within the architecture of human mercy for my now begun and ongoing restitution.

As a fourteen year old I had left my great-grandfather's school when the Sun at noon began quiet but desolate keenings in the sky above the Guianas and the God-Ship of Chaos filled a monstrous berth in the iron stanchions of the Demerara River. I left with the at-that-time light but unportionable burden of my great-grandfather's spiritual decimation-in-living that had taken furious abode, though it had still fully to accomplish itself in his flesh: a decimation that would take another decade fully to consummate.

Furies of the flesh and fatal fating in the young body of black Demerara water continued to hide the catastrophic collapse of pre-Columbian civilisations below the calm discharge from the banks of the river. Rotting banks of river continued to draw down and shed into the impassive currents their intimate masonic correspondence with a lost consciousness that had part-petrified in the sudden and confounding Amerindian petro-glyphs that are the radio-isotope emitters in the geography of the Guianas: brilliant coloured rock paintings undisclosed in the forest hinter-land, and maddeningly hinted at in the degraded *articrafts* of vestige-survivors from pre- and post-Columbian decimations.

(As indigenous peoples, Amerindians uncan-nily map their broken gene-line in the banded and helical straw of their Tibi-series basket-weaving, in the same way, for instance, that native American polychrome baskets are deco-rated with the beta-helix of bacterial rubredoxin; or the lightning pattern of chicken-muscle pro-teins appears on the Anasazi Indian redware pitchers; or the geometric border of the red-figured amphora holds the "Greek key" struc-ture of human prealbumin.)

That unclarified reserve-put-on-unauctioned-goods I carried in me as I left my great-grandfa-ther's schoolhouse. I was expected to go straight home along the sparse community of the riverbank then up the trailing sandy hill, but I walked into time-lapses of footprints and an involuntary asso-ciation with disappearing creatures, or rather of creatures who flit half-seen within the rhythms of walking, which appear among the unrecorded monuments and prowl and haunt the esplanade and pediments of cultural memory.

That whole reserve was in my satchel. I did not know how I could reach home carrying that heaviness. I thought of what I could plausibly tell my grandmother: that the satchel was stolen, or of how a bigger boy roughed me up and took it, or it slipped off my shoulder and fell in the river, or my great-grandfather had said that he would bring it like a trophy when next he rode his minotaur-bicycle to the entrance of our maze. Indeed, the satchel became so heavy that I could no longer lift it off the ground and my footprints began to sink below the surface of the road.

We had been sent home early because it was Independence Day. I.D.-Day, May 26th, nineteen hundred and sixty-six, a day of masque when the temporary landlords conceded political autonomy to the tenants' association. My own fact of being is partly such a colonization of the temporal, and I am like a guest overlooked in the invitation list, who turns up anyway, identifies himself and is admitted with the formal words of welcome.

"Yuh welcome here, Leon. Mos' welcome. Bring you'self in. Yuh with your mati here, eh."

"I am glad that you have not excluded me," I stammered. "I appreciate how busy you've been and how much you've had to look over. Even in a family, essential things get overlooked. Indeed, what it is to be of the human family! Also, I'm especially glad in another oblique way. You see, *InterDependence* is the event of the day. Nothing else is so prominent in the racial diary. Had I not gained entry here I would have been obliged to go to a more obscure meeting out in the bush with souls whose names I do not rightly know, and join in with ceremonies whose protocol might build confusing bridges across territories of estrangedness. I might be asked perhaps to anchor my floating rib in a new anatomy of identity and to induce a birth of hard self-knowledge and, more obscurely, cultural salvation. Yes, it is good to be here among the light and liquor, the fast women and the slow dances. Thank you so very much indeed."

I was not to have this recourse. The Sun was a harsh tether. It flayed the tongue of muscular water and accentuated the closeness of the creatures of between-dimensions, so that they began to interrupt my stride even as I was sinking thigh-deep into the road.

May 26th, nineteen hundred and sixty-six. *Identity Day* into whose uncanny umbilicus of road I seemed to be reabsorbed. For reasons then not recognised by myself, Half-Mile Road was empty except for me. Why had I left the schoolhouse so much after everybody else? Had I myself, a fourteen-year old, closed the school's double wooden door and stepped so unprotected into the gods' solarium?

May or month of Roman Maia, goddess of growth and increase. In Gaelic: *Mios bochuin* – the Month of Swelling; in Anglo-Saxon: *Thrimilci* – the month when cows give milk thrice a day, the dairy month. Dairy, a room where bread is made from milk-dough. Old English *dag*, dough, and Old Norse *deigja*, dairymaid or kneader of bread from dough.

But what had the Roman calendar to do with the deep geology of this land? Through what fissures does the buried calendar of unrecorded indigenes continue to erupt and breach the macadamisations of successive colonies? Why did the carnival masks of Independence celebration have no faces for this hidden history of tongues-between-utterances, those creatures of silences that were making themselves my travelling companions?

I missed the turning home. Everywhere was deserted. The road continued me past my path home, past the church of St. Aidan Martyr of aluminium spire & spiritual gridiron, past the stelling for the ferry boats crossing to Port MacKenzie, past the pastor's paschal house, the cake shop, the dice-shed and rum shop, and out of my known geography. Why had the road been so empty? On my right, the river grew turbulent. Wismar Hill, which I should have taken, receded on the left. The cleft in which I was walking had gradually deepened and my head was all but level with the road. The carrion smell, the droppings and the occasional growling of the heavy beasts were very close. The large cats flitted in and out of view, but I could distinctly feel the contours of their bodies as they brushed time and again against me. The road had been surfaced with heavy red bauxite dust that squalled and covered my face in a warm, thick, ochre layer. Thus masked, I left behind me the settlement of Wismar and a little further down the river entered the graveyard at Christianburg.

What is the hidden calendar of these events? Which unrecorded gods, 'big men' and animals have lent their names and character to sunken civilisations that pile up like shipwrecks in the tidal harbour?

Successive tides uncover and reveal hidden potentialities in burial. The God-Ship of Chaos, whose hull distends with greed, in turn becomes candidate for the boat-bone breaker's yard. Why did I go into the graveyard at Christianburg if not to survive war? War of Want. War of Dependence. War against Conscience. War that slew every nine and passed over the tenth (whose inverse decimation was involving my great-grandfather). The war of dogmas that was putting larger and larger overseas Dependencies into annex while at the same time plundering them and willing consent with apparatuses such as the Chortling-God Ship of Chaos which was laughing all the way to the Bank of Demerara – apparatuses of State banking on Ships of Rapacious Laughter.

Gassed by laughter, burial became for many a turning up of enriched soil by consanguineous souls who could no longer stand their ground. The graveyard at Christianburg was heaped with the dead. Piles and piles of soldier's corpses dressed in green. They lay in casual heaps on the ground. They made hummocks about the burial ground. They made fleshly barrows. I understood with the directness of intuition that while I could not liberate the world they failed to defend, I could at least choose eventual liberation for myself. I thought that the road, whose cleft was now healing and raising me back above the ground level, would lead me to a new consecration of unfathomable ground. Only now do I begin to articulate the origins and conjunctions I myself became, arching me out of the graveyard, across a wide fresh stream, to a nurturing bank.

First make an inventory of what we can of the irreparable. Psychologically this is a job for a trickster & twin who keep on fluking what truly cannot be reversed. (Would I find my footprints in Wismar-Linden today, which were disappearing even as I was walking down the riverside road as a fourteen-year old?) Although Guyanese soldiers of five hues and colour served in the Great War of 1914-18 as the infamously shamed eight thousand strong British West Indian Regiment, and came out again for the North African War of 1940-1943, the newly heaped dead were not the fallen of the Great Wars but were the young and green of the hidden calendar, forced to appropriate the costume of contemporary combatants if they were to inspire at least commemoration. Why commemorate what you have no direct link with?

Memory is a genealogy grown out of land, a means of making loss survivable, and thus of allowing what is past to have closure. Unless we rebuild for the lost genealogies, we contribute to the disinitiatives in memory and feelings that fate us into the role of unknowing victims to the invisible hand of decimation.

The young and green dead of the hidden forest hunter & gatherer calendar are an embodiment of the protracted and unresolved matter touched on when speaking of what it is to be transplanted to an already inhabited continent. We get a contrasting sense of this if we consider settlement in a parallel space to Guyana: the British Isles.

Prehistory in the British Isles is ringed with giants whose earthworks – mounds, standing stones, barrows – have left prominent and cogent organs in the land. Compare the tonal continuity of these phrases in geologue with the discontinuity of sign, for instance, in the acute bombardments of the recent Second War. Whereas all traces of war damage to cities such as London and Coventry had been effaced by the early nineteen sixties (that totality of destruction inspiring an even stronger instinct for renewal) a flight over the English mid-western shires (Avebury, Silbury, West Kennet) reveals ancient articulate prehistories, terraforms or shapings-in-earth, whose language is coherent because most can read it, and whose literacy the nation has preserved in protected sites, museums, and land held in trust for the nation. Albion's giants have, though, left no remnant of indigenous peoples to be accommodated in the modern world!

By contrast, pre- and post-Colombian histories of the rainforest hunter & gatherer calendar of South America exhibit a chronic and oblique reflex: successive decimation followed by protracted continuance. The descendents of the ancient indigenes protract with time. Whereas in the postwar rebuilding of London, for instance, effacement of an immediate past was given proportion by the nation's continuance with a *chorea gigantum* or nativity-star of legacy-with-giants, in South America, commemorials of prehistory are prevented by mutism or legacies that remain unreadable – chiefly by South America's scenario as the unique continent to which man is not a native species.

Between 1,200 and 500 BC, Olmec progenitors of pre-Columbian civilizations created a style of numeracy and hieroglyph that would seed the entire continent. They sculpted meso-America with ceremonial stone. They let loose into the imagination the cult of puma, ocelot and jaguar. In their name, the Maya would fit a stark ship of conquest and human sacrifice whose shadow would touch their hunter-gatherer brethren circum-Caribbean, in the islands, the Guianas and the Amazonian watershed. It would rig a strange *vulnerus* in the Nomad Calendar.

My cousin-german, cousin of my heart, Elizabeth-Eberhardt Bethesda, reappeared to me. Over time, Elizabeth-E Bethesda had become achingly familiar to me without me being able quite to account for how we should have grown so close together. We had not spent prolonged time with one another, yet she reappears from time to time in my life to put her hand on my shoulder and walk a little way with me in an uncanny apprehension of my state and need. Elizabeth-E Bethesda had an intimate correspondence with the moon when it quits its orbit and walks on the Earth as the familiar of men. She was born in Silver City on the Wismar side of the Demerara. Her house stands back on a leafy avenue and in the yard is an abundant argentine Year Tree. On this, the most recent occasion, she had joined me in the deepening road between the church of St. Aidan's Martyr and my entry into Christianburg. Elizabeth Bethesda is, to my memory, tall, leggy, dark, affectionate. I know her also for being fair and bright and laughing.

She had leant her head on my shoulder and for a moment closed her eyes against the unburied mounds of bodies, the illiteracy in the young and green calendar of slaughter. An uncanny termination in the bridge of survival, whistling and fluting its convergent arch from Olmec meso-America and Maya dominance, to the circum-Caribbean Carib reign of terror, to the religious hegemony of the Andean centre of Chavin de Huantar, then from the Mexico valley, and already rumoured in the oblique illuminated register of Aztec Montezuma, to the eventual messianic return of Quetzalcoatl-Hernan Cortez, had made a strange prognosis for my individual release from ending.

I left the graveyard and crossed the short bridge to Roseland Park (it was at that moment Elizabeth-E Bethesda had rested her head on my shoulder and closed her eyes) but for reasons I did not then understand I turned back to the bridge. On the pavement were gathered many people, as if lining the route of a parade or a fete. Indeed they parted way for a riderless horse, a sorrel stallion, which galloped across the bridge from the cemetery-side past me. Where had the people come from? The town and the main road in Wismar had been deserted. Had these people been waiting here since noon for the sorrel horse, moving and heavy with the remembrance of other dreams? Had it somehow been anticipated that here, on the border of rich parkland, the sorrel stallion would be joined by a mare with whom he would race into the stream, with whom he would disport, and whom he would mount in sexual embrace?

The mane of bridge, its bridle of stone, curb of pavement, cheek-strap and truss, the riding of its slight camber, flowed half-seen within the contours of adjacent histories. The long coarse hairs in the Bridge of Mane strung a musical bow in the intense *essai* of Lorenzo Hervas y Panduro's *Idea dell' universo* (1778-87). The horse's flanks were taut with the ethnology or knowledge of the race against disappearance. His nostrils were saline with oceans, tidal inland seas and sudden encounters with the feline carnivores on history's pathfinding.

I had left my great-grandfather's schoolhouse when the Sun was in keenest glossochronia. It had been suffixing noon with the Amerindian languages of Guyana – with Arawak, Atorai, Mapidian, Wapishana, Chiquena, and Caribe. It had begun to beckon a different character to Independence Day.

The road had seemed empty to me because the carnival face of Independence Celebration had neither the contours nor the suggestion of features for unrecorded indigenous histories, and this had made the independence celebrants invisible to me. To commute with inner or unacknowledged time (the to-this-day still ongoing swinging-close of the high wooden doors of the school house) I had become the *filius unius diei*, son of one day who would cross into Roseland Park with solar horses.

Only moments had passed since the surge of peoples and the horses of marathon that brought the character of fury to the bridging point. The noise and excitement of the independence crowd, expressed in creole gestures and the declamations of six peoples taking possession of a 'country of garden places', appeared experimental to a living yet undiscovered intertidal text. Traditions of perspective were being confounded by the complex patternings that constantly transgressed their apparent frame, as though aligning themselves within hidden and inexplicable calendars.

It gave that odour of apprehension so well known to peoples who find themselves come into sudden possession of countries, administrations and resources of great potential: a glut condition that unaccountably shadows the hand of plenty so that each act of recognition becomes an agnostic gesture.

It is possible that the crowd were none other than the dismounted riders of the sorrel horses, each man and woman and child formulating simultaneously the single gesture of *cabellos desaparecos* or dismissal from a chivalric liturgy.

I paused in sudden possession of all lapses or conscriptions into hidden resource, like one who turns aside into the Inn of Horses at noon, myself in auto-portrait with bridleless horse, myself modelled equally as child-adult child-woman child-man. Do not imagine that I identified with the bridleless horses. I must consider the fact that I might have been too unconscious or tranced to notice my own lifting of the bridle. Through me the gesture of *desapareco* threatened to continue itself. I moved apart from the dismounted riders and considered whether to go down to the water to wash the rowan mask of red bauxite dust from my face, but I was already turning away from the unhorsed people, and was running into Roseland Park; there, though, the unmasking-by-water or baptismal gesture of disinvestment never reached my face but became, instead, one of unexpected conciliation.

Roseland Park was filled with deer that left their browsing, surrounded me, and thrust their long muzzles into my palm. Running, I had become aware of having stretched out my arms behind me, and of the oblique rotation of my palms outward from my body. Did such a motion, my own outward turning of palms to nurture the deer in Roseland Park, not ghost the messianic gestures of conciliation or point to the divine that is in the creaturely body? Did the sign not seek to heal the future rupture in communion that the tidal wave caused; a communion we had been holding not inside the church building but out of doors, along the canal, on the brickdam wall looking out to where Laban had erected an altar-on-water in the Ark he had assembled, and which stood in El Doradean isolation in the middle of the reservoir as if he, Jacob-Israel Laban – the limping promised-land gilded man – was journeying to us, as if to a far shore, to dust us with the gold in his skin?

It was a possibility that tormented me in my sleep. The shimmer of water laminated my cocoon in mud-limes that were wafer-thin and golden. The labour of my dilatory breaths, which were causing the cocoon to shudder, might have been a reflex in myself anticipating sudden submersion, the way a deep-sea diver might prepare himself for apnoea, or it might have been signalling a deliberate and perhaps malicious slowing down by Amalivacar through the night bush. Why would Amalivacar slow down if not to deepen the graduations in the soul, or was he listening closely as well, the way one listens when one is straining to hear the approach of dread?

It was then that Amalivacar first spoke directly to me.

"Such an approach, Leon-Battista, is fraught with uncertainty, restraint. We have to endure, as our constant, our own partial access to the events that live us. We can no longer labour under the illusion of the impartial. At every step and turn we have to acknowledge just how discontinuous is consciousness within the intuitive fabric of hybrid culture, hybrid psyche and hybrid cosmos."

"Are we not haunted," I replied to my rescuing god, "by the community of our unlived selves? Are we not also possessed by an inherent rigidity that entombs us in unilateral stances in far-reaching decisions (the voting and vetoing of the one thing or the other). That rigidity also stops us from making crucial connections between spheres of learning, spheres of mutual influence, the music of the spheres and relocated environments in overlapping theatres and layers of memory and futuring books of being. It is rigidity that hems us in to the stern logic of fate and the predetermined ends of tragedy. An epoch that speaks of the death of tragedy speaks, in a way, of its own demise. As post-tragedians we continue a limbo of melodrama and in this way die many unregistered deaths. Rigidity, then, keeps us outside register." I sighed.

I was being held down in the dirt of the market square. A cloth was put in my mouth to keep me from swallowing my tongue (after six years I had become a well-known figure of a fool) and was bound with a vibrant luminous cord to keep me from harming myself.

That luminous cord held the vibrant harmonics by which the Sun had hitched himself to me when, as a fourteen-year old, I spent the day in his solarium. Since that day, had I not spent my life climbing a ladder of scale up and down from heaven? The constellations in my dream-book of unlived selves compose their sweet harrowing music in the windy roaring chambers of space. They sing fierce and gentle messages that I will need to continue interpreting into infinity, into new conceptions of myself that seem to precede me and with which I wrestle almost blindly.

I now deduce with the hindsight of restored memory that those herald's messages may have been at their strongest precisely during the period of amnesia as they recombined me for a new basis in life, and that they might have had to defer or suspend my memory of my own person during the period of recombination. It was the corded agency of the rope that laid this possibility open to me as I lay bound in the dirt, the opening exertion of recovered memory rushing on me with exhilarating urgency....

The day spent in the gods' solarium did not simply end with my feeding the deer in Roseland Park. As I lay frothing on the dirt of Mackenzie Market my mind's eye rescued as from a *camera lucida* the sexual embrace of the mare and sorrel stallion on Independence Day 1966. The two horses had waded into the swift, soft-contouring stream, their necks and heads lying one over and next to the other, and as I watched, the horses anthropomorphised into an elderly human couple in loving embrace, an old virile happy couple with the aspect of royalty, him wearing Sol's cap and her, Dame Selina's silvery bonnet. Sol glanced back over his shoulder and winked at me.

Yes, Sol's lusty wink was the prelude to my entering Roseland Park and my first conscious acquaintance with the unwritten gamut of inherencies in which I was to find myself suspended....

The pictograms impressed in my skin by the fleet love-child made taut the cord stretched from the Sun to me. It was the medium in which the pictograms were fixed that pushed me into the sailing corridors of resuscitated space. The glyphs were dyed in human skin. Cicatriced skin. O Happy Day!

I had been badly cut trying to evade Forbes' knives when, disguised as the Whistling Man, he came at me as I was struggling to get free of my bed and the tenting of the mosquito net. The knives had struck and the skin had come away, yet so gorged was I with movement that I did not notice the cut at first.

Amalivacar had somehow got hold of the fallen skin. The pictograms had been composed on the skin that had once covered the raw weeping area over my solar plexus and had never healed over since the accident at Manchester. The skin had been exquisitely treated and preserved. The dye in it must have been introduced with painstaking care at the ends of unimaginably fine needle points.

Once begun, the clarifications increased in pressure. As I lay in my mud-lair evading rescue and lapsing in and out of sight of Amalivacar, I had noticed a certain purple patch stuck to his ribs that seemed alien and opaque on his body. I could not at the time read it for it appeared discoloured and thickened, as if an attempt at healing post-operative trauma. Now at last I saw it for what it was. Amalivacar was wearing the fallen skin from my own body!

The bridge which connected the stripping of my skin to its new position among the epigraphs on Amalivacar's is what returned my memory to me. That stripping of skins laid bare over time bowled me over. I began to augur and divine with the dust in which I lay at Mackenzie Market. I lay in the eye of a storm of fish scales and fruit skins and vegetable peelings that shuddered as I shuddered. I saw Laban stand beside a sinister, culling organ that sought to deepen the abyss out of which the tidal wave of futuring glimpses had struck the Manchester ark.

I had wished for Death's sting to make me immune to future death, to free me from the tragedy of further unregistered deaths. Each numbing sting would leave a star or 'anaesthesia to sensation' on the carapace of my body. It would fill my body with stars or nodes of non-sensation. Channels and canals and solar tunnels between the numbings or hibernations would eventually anastomose to form a new constellation, a new conception of consciousness in the body. It would change my nature without me being able to feel it. It would bring about a non-sensational change in my human nature that would lie obdurately in the cleft of the sensational world. Such had been my death wish.

It seems to me that the body is a hollowed chamber upon whose surfaces might accrete subjects superimposed from the universe. We live in sketches; allow faint tracings of ourselves over the forms we can make out in creation. We live a precarious sacrament that is vulnerable to acts of violence. It is necessary to suspend the acts of judgement that are the prelude to violence; tribal pacts with which the world dominates and destroys species of being it cannot fathom.

My ligature with the Sun began to lose its incendiary character. Through the dreaming door in the ground of Mackenzie Market I began to discern a subterranean court, a sunken arena and an archaeology of figures wearing mask-like expressions and continuing a cryptic ceremony among upright blades of jade. I did not need an inner eye to recognise that I looked on the hidden progenitors of the Americas and the 'vestments in nature' they would borrow: the Weeping god, the Smiling god, the Staff god, the Jaguar god. 'Vestments in nature' serve to conserve patterns of behaviour in the land. Expeditions into the deep rainforests of Guyana uncover fragmented, perishable texts left by the Arawaks, the Macusi, and the Warraus. These indigenous peoples claim that the landscape is a living organism that moves, that speaks, that acts on man. When we analyse the deprivations of Amerindian, then European, empires, we understand that the acts which past inhabitants commit in the land become the reflex acts of the newcomers who try to settle it.

The new settlers seem to be forced into chronic or historic patterns of behaviour, behaviours that seem to be imposed on them, by the land itself.

'Vestments in nature' serve to conserve patterns of behaviour in the land. The new conception of ourselves will reinvest the gods.

As I mused this, Amalivacar broke out of the circle of avatars in the hidden court below the ground of Mackenzie market and I had to swing my head around into the piloting & parallel space of Manchester the better to see him approach through the night bush. My helpers in the market place must have thought me in the throes of a fit, but all I was doing was moving my head to follow Amalivacar.

When one names creation in oneself, creation in the advocate, creation in the plaintiff and delugee, creation in the wrestling, limping, promised-land gilded self, the archeology of memory can be recovered. It is a mercy and reprieve afforded by the recovering-traditions of the arts of the imagination; traditions that recover me; traditions that remain provisional though nonetheless powerful. We are torn between the institutionalising of a literate, coherent and historicised tradition, and traditions of the imagination that make an exception of history, that stand outside our expectations for formal historic coherence; traditions of the arts of the imagination which abolish the absolute premise of race and geopolitics and instead mediate a hidden capacity in the 'body of civilisation' to portray, in layered ancestries, an opening into the layered evolution of a victor who saves lives, who rescues us from the predatory logic of conquest...

The rustling in Elizabeth-Eberhardt's twisting serpentine turn on the Manchester ark had launched a multitude of rainbows in the spray and crest of the wave front. The ark sprang vertically upward fifty feet or more to ride the incoming tide, the water-line marked in clear ruddle; a red-line over which the tide should not pass, a red-line for a red-letter day.

In advanced equations there is bound to be a certain decommissioning of real figures. We replace them with tiny compact letter-notations embodying entire processes in the hope that they will not burst their discrete packets. We quantise them against the spillages inevitable in multitude assemblies. It was the ruddle chalk Elizabeth-Eberhardt had dropped and for which she seemed to be searching, as if for something, in the cockpit of the moon, and it was to recover the lapsed ruddle chalk that Amalivacar had broken out of the circle of avatars in the hidden archeology of memory and begun his staggered, wiggly path through the night bush.

The tidal wave engulfed villages, back-dams, reservoirs, and rice-farms. When I last glimpsed the ark, thronging with fragile humanity, it was sailing serenely into the mountain of water, a cavern open-ing to accommodate the bulk of the ark in the sheltering harbour of the water mountain.

Laban stood in the stern waving and, I fancied, grinning at me. The day-Moon ascended and stood directly above the breaking wave. Solar winds rushed out from the Sun, pushed their branching brachiate fires through the recesses of space. These converged into roots, trunk and stem of a world tree that was forming behind the Moon. The willow tree of the world possessed an abundance of cascading tendrils. In each were lodged unusual winking lights that gradually showed themselves to be the pilot-lights of spatial vessels. The weeping, sighing, smiling Aaron's tree of world was none other than a harbour for vessels of deep-space that, ascended from the moon, could lodge and resource themselves there. Through its harrowing of time and cultural institution (the Mass, masquerade, native host sensibilities in the Americas) the Ark of Manchester had gained a berth in the world tree.

Two nights later, when Amalivacar broke from the forest, the waters were placid. Manchester village was submerged fathoms below on a new bed or buried compass in the Guyanese Atlantic. Amalivacar had stripped naked and was putting on a diver's helmet to begin his descent to the submerged Manchester village. He would look for the dropped ruddle chalk to carry back to his court so that ever newer and more experimental water-lines might be affixed to future covenants with consciousness in the archaeology of memory. He would liberate me from the mud-sleeve. He would touch my forehead briefly with the ruddle chalk as he returned.

Amalivacar's wandering planetary course in the night bush is a telling entry in the nomad calendar of surviving hunter & gathering forest peoples. The fluidity of rocks, trees, skies and forest resonates with a certain 'valour and voice' that enables us to recognise these parables of being in the language of the stars and the moon. The nocturnal sky is exceedingly impressive to one who navigates by night. It holds an architecture of consciousness in the apparent *vulnerus* in the nomad calendar in the instances where a nomad would leave no permanent signs of culture and no template of the imagination. If this were not so, Elizabeth would not have been able to show me, many light years hence, pulsars and gamma-busters in an epoch where the stars would no longer be seen as abstract notations of space but as a relocated centre of creativity. It is an imaginative resource, in our present age, obscurely lodged in the host cosmologies of peoples of nomadic culture, to whom the Pleiades ("the granary") the Orqo-Cilay ("the multicoloured llama") the Yutu-yutu (partridge-like bird) are known and named in the cincture of the Milky Way and its adjacent interstellar clouds and reproduced in the ground plan of living spaces and communities on the Earth.

The Ark of Manchester ascends to the Moon as a spacecraft and recesses to dock on the world-tree at the same time as it lies submerged in the new sunken harbour of Manchester village. In accommodating both events, we free ourselves from the suffocated breath lines made by the irrigation of coastal land that along with the exploited forests and oil-rich territories feeds the actual and ongoing, often rapacious, conquest in the Americas.

"You are not exempt," Amalivacar whispered to me, "You are not exempt."

I felt my eyes bolt, show their whites. "Am I to continue to be conquered?" I started, fearful. "How much rape must the soul endure? After all this time, is it not enough?"

"You are an instrument of passion, Leon-Battista," Amalivacar murmured.

"Nails protrude from the fingers of the bishop as indices of passion," I answered. "Nails, art-god. I know that I am not as hard as nails."

The passionate avatar hesitated as if turning over the findings in an archive. He shook his head and I knew that he too had heard the brief tearing and rending flesh in the subsiding carnival of Manchester village. We both heard it in the leaves and branches of the world tree. The world tree trembled.

"Something has to give way at some level or other, Leon-Battista; some value, which may be apparently eclipsed or apparently buried in history, but which might still be alive, has to find me. Because I am navigating blind in a variable reed boat, I am variable with sleep and sight and am vulnerable to dream. The rhythms and inflexions of dream overtake me and I begin to dream my own conundrum, I begin to dream the conundrum of eclipsed value: thus the thing that must give way at some level gestates in my dream. I am asleep and it is awake. I am in dream-sleep and it is in waking-eclipse. Is this not masque?"

I shook my head and it tilted suddenly forward with its heavy bill. I shook out my tarred & albioned cheek-feathers. I groomed them fleetingly with the three nails of my sloth's claw.

"I think I am understanding," I offered, "although that is never enough. I am not exempt. I lay in a submerged landscape above the ancient floor of the ocean with its abrupt cliffs, veined rock, fossil brush, buried plantations; their lines of flow indifferent to pathway as to barrier. Do I look to borrow a master-sense for things that appear to go against sense?"

"It is an effort, Leon-Battista, a marking by timehrian hands from out of the imagination. Consider: are we not like harvesters on the sea bed clearing plants, a crane-like lung technology beside us, a combining of unfathomable resources in intangible being?"

Leon-Battista Mondaal
Wismar-MacKenzie
Demerara County, Guyana
since 1st January, 1991.